Keepers of the House

Also by Lisa St Aubin de Terán:

Novels
The Slow Train to Milan
The Tiger
The Bay of Silence
Black Idol
Joanna
Nocturne
The Palace
Otto

Memoirs
Off the Rails: Memoirs of a Train Addict
A Valley in Italy: Confessions of a House Addict
The Hacienda: My Venezuelan Years
Memory Maps
Mozambique Mysteries

Short stories
The Marble Mountain
Southpaw

Poetry
The High Place

Travelogue
Venice: The Four Seasons

Edited anthologies
Indiscreet Journeys: Stories of Women on the Road
Virago Book of Wanderlust and Dreams
Elements of Italy

Keepers of the House

Lisa St Aubin de Terán

amaurea

ISBN 978-1-914278-15-0 (hardback)
ISBN 978-1-914278-16-7 (paperback)
ISBN 978-1-914278-17-4 (eBook)

First published 1982 by Jonathan Cape (ISBN 9780224020015)
2nd edition 1994, Bloomsbury Modern Classics (ISBN 9780747517429)

This new edition published in Great Britain by Amaurea Press 2024

British Library Catalogue in Publishing Data
A catalogue record for this book is available from the British Library.

Cover, book design & typesetting by Albarrojo

Amaurea Press is an imprint of Amaurea Creative Productions Ltd.
London, United Kingdom
www.amaurea.co.uk

To Jaime Terán

and Benito Mendoza

...When the keepers of the house shall tremble, and the strong men shall bow themselves, and the grinders cease because they are few, and those that look out of the windows be darkened... Also when they shall be afraid of that which is high, and fears shall be in the way, and the almond tree shall flourish, and the grasshopper shall be a burden, and desire shall fail: because man goeth to his long home, and the mourners go about the streets: ... Then shall the dust return to the earth as it was...

Ecclesiastes 12: 3-7

CONTENTS

Rodrigo Beltrán m Rosa de Labastida de Labastida
1760-1840

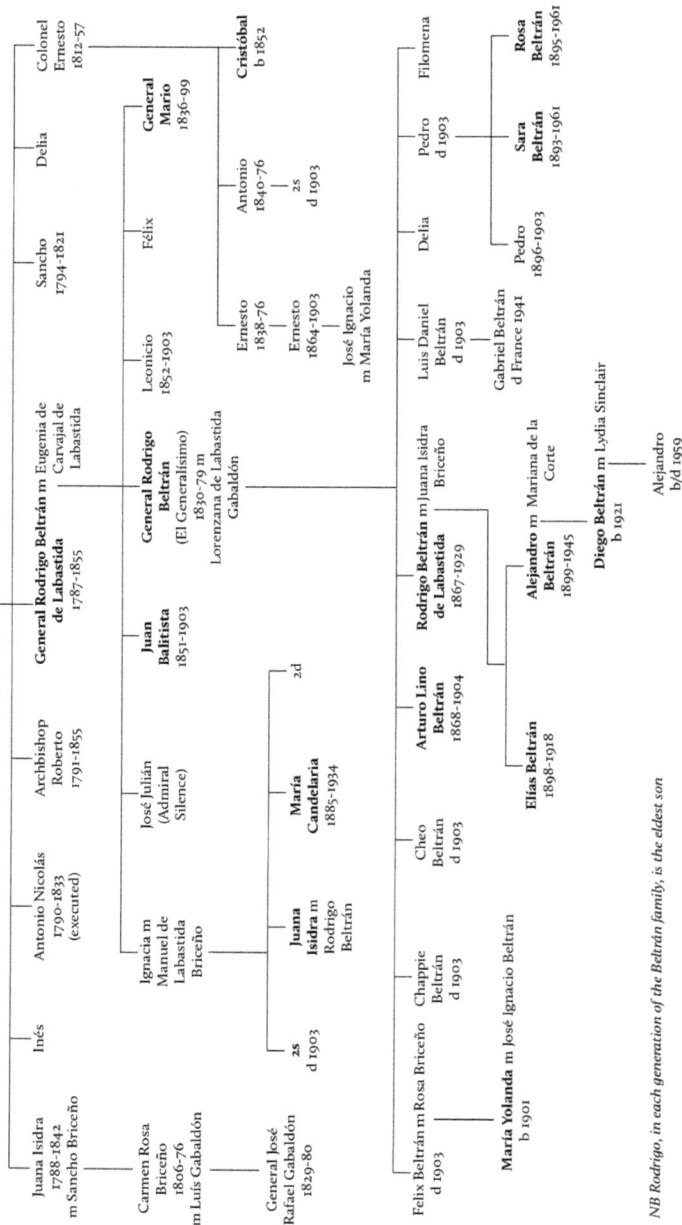

Juana Isidra 1788-1842 m Sancho Briceño — Inés — Antonio Nicolás 1790-1833 (executed) — Archbishop Roberto 1791-1855 — **General Rodrigo Beltrán de Labastida** 1787-1855 — Sancho 1794-1821 — Delia — Colonel Ernesto 1812-57

Carmen Rosa Briceño 1806-76 m Luís Gabaldón — José Julián (Admiral Silence) — Ignacia m Manuel de Labastida Briceño — **General Rodrigo Beltrán** (El Generalísimo) 1830-79 m Lorenzana de Labastida Gabaldón — **Juan Baltista** 1851-1903 — Leonicio 1852-1903 — Félix — **General Mario** 1836-99 — **Cristóbal** b 1852

General José Rafael Gabaldón 1829-80 — 2s d 1903 — Juana Isidra m Rodrigo Beltrán — **María Candelaria** 1885-1934 (2d) — Ernesto 1838-76 — Ernesto 1864-1903 — José Ignacio m María Yolanda — Antonio 1840-76 (2s) d 1903

Felix Beltrán m Rosa Briceño d 1903 — Chappie Beltrán d 1903 — Cheo Beltrán d 1903 — **Arturo Lino Beltrán** 1868-1904 — **Rodrigo Beltrán de Labastida** 1867-1929 m Juana Isidra Briceño — Luis Daniel Beltrán d 1903 — Filomena — Delia — Pedro d 1903 — **Sara Beltrán** 1893-1961 — **Rosa Beltrán** 1895-1961 — Pedro 1896-1903 — Gabriel Beltrán d France 1941

Elias Beltrán 1898-1918 — **Alejandro** m Mariana de la Corte **Beltrán** 1899-1945 — **Diego Beltrán** m Lydia Sinclair b 1921

María Yolanda m José Ignacio Beltrán b 1901

Alejandro b/d 1959

NB Rodrigo, in each generation of the Beltrán family, is the eldest son

PROLOGUE

I

L YDIA Sinclair was just seventeen when she arrived on her husband's estate in the Andes, and from the first day she felt that she belonged there. She had never felt that she belonged anywhere before that. She could remember being sent out to play, aged five, on a day when her family had just moved house in London. Her mother and half-sisters were arranging furniture and books, while she held onto a drainpipe and swung gently from side to side watching some children playing nearby. It was then she realised that she was not like anyone else. She repeated it to herself that morning, 'I am different, I am different, I am different.' The thought stayed with her as a lump in her throat until she reached the Hacienda La Bebella, where she thought: 'I belong.'

Her first day went by in a haze of mosquito bites and heat and a swarm of new faces. The farm workers and visitors saw her swathed in a long dress and with a wide-brimmed hat, and were struck by her likeness to the tall women who had lived in the valley before her time. The children laughed a little at her strangeness and the sheer height of her, but the older ones recognised in her a vision of the past, and they were full of hope for what she might do.

Lydia was pleased and excited by the countryside with its shadowy green slopes, and frangipani flowers spiking out of the higher rocks. Her house was like a tumbledown palace with its arches and balconies, and gigantic cedar beams criss-crossing the ceiling of every room. One end of the house crouched like a hare under the mountain; the other overlooked the River Momboy. During the hot afternoons she would lie in an old embroidered hammock. It had belonged to her father-in-law, like many things there, for, despite his having died eighteen years before, the house was full of him. It was very much his house, and her husband was always referred to as 'Don Alejandro's son'. She herself began there as Doña Lydia, but quickly became La Doña as though there were no other; and her name was never heard again outside her own room.

The whole estate was badly neglected when she arrived, but, after the first few months, when her husband, Diego, took an interest in the running of the Hacienda, she soon learned how to put things in order. The rings and pouches under Diego's eyes had grown and stayed, and his natural tendency to sleep at every opportunity was exaggerated by a new malfunction of his kidneys, which Benito dosed with a potion that he brewed himself from the savage *ñongue* plant. Perched on her horse, or striding in high boots through the grass, Lydia reviewed the fields like an officer his troops. Her aide-de-camp was a large scraggynecked turkey vulture who followed her everywhere in blind adoration. He was called Napoleon, on account of his military pose. The bird had been a present from an eccentric friend of her husband's who had given him to her in an unseemly hessian sack, saying,

'Take him, Doña, he'll soon settle down with you.'

She had opened the sack and the bird had flapped out and hidden in the undergrowth behind the house. When she had stooped to pick him up, his curved black beak had twisted in a death clasp around her wrist.

'Hold him tight, Doña,' the man had cried, 'he doesn't want to wound you.'

She had laboured with the pain, while the blood drained from her hand. Then Napoleon had let go, and neither of them had known who held whom. The vulture had arrived on her second day; on her third day, an old man called Natividad had hobbled up to her to tell her that his only daughter had left him for a man with a donkey, and that he would live on his own now. Lydia had been at a loss for words, so she had nodded and watched him go wheezing back to his empty hut. There seemed to be no escape from the sound of his wheezing, which the wind carried down the hill to drift up around her house.

She took her bearings and adjusted herself to the Momboy valley with the same ease with which she had adjusted herself to the hammock. It was particularly easy for her to think, stretched out flat between the two pillars that supported her. She liked to feel herself enclosed by greatness, rocking between extremes. It was the extremes that first attracted her to her husband, Don Diego Beltrán. She had been fascinated by his debauched good looks and his pride. They had met in London, when she was sixteen and he was thirty-five. He had found her there, and followed her, and by his constant presence she had come to love him. He had been like a great rare fish washed ashore, whose lungs had been unable to adapt to the twentieth century. It was the first time that he had ever left the Andes, and had he not been exiled for political offences, he would never have left them at all. But he had landed in London, and fallen in love with Lydia as a schoolgirl in love with the past, and after two years of honeymoon in Italy he had taken her back to what he always referred to as his 'little place in the Andes'. To Diego it may have seemed like a little place, coming as he did from a family who had once owned every mountain range from Trujillo to Mérida and on over the icy *páramo* to Pamplona and across the plains of the Orinoco to Barinas and Niquitao. But to his wife, Lydia, the 'little place' was a vast estate, such as she had never seen before, where the sugarcane stretched for as far as the eye could see along the valley, and grove after grove of avocados clung to the terraced slopes of the surrounding hills.

Diego and Lydia had what was really more of an understanding than a marriage. Even when Lydia's Spanish had become second nature to her, they spoke very little, because Diego was an unusually silent man. It was only when he talked about the Hacienda, or about the past, that he shone as a conversationalist, and he had only spleen to vent on the time being with its bought power and its petrol dollar and its war on the environment. So the estate became the missing link in their silent marriage, and 'the family' assumed the life that Diego lacked. He was more like his ancestors than any other member of the family, and despite his present apathy had done more to change its future. However, all his plans had aborted one after the other, like a machine gun fire of miscarriages.

Diego divided his time between sleeping and reading, and he would spend every day either in his rooms or locked in the upstairs library, where the shelves of tattered leather volumes were always thick with the crumbled remains of bookworms and cockroaches and paper dust. Sometimes he would visit what was left of his family, in ritualised rounds in the neighbouring town, some fifteen miles away. And Lydia would be left on her own. For company, there were Benito Mendoza, who was eighty-nine and had worked for the family since he was a boy; the beagle hounds that she had brought over with her on the ship from England; and four girls to help in the house.

The girls were mostly shy and silent with her, but they chattered endlessly among themselves, and they seemed to have forgotten everything that they had learned from their mothers except how to soak clothes: the rambling house was filled with little bowls of stale suds, forgotten and mouldering under beds and tables. Eventually the girls were succeeded by an old housekeeper, and a child, who was her cousin, to help her. Benito bickered with the old lady, who was called La Comadre Matilde, and proposed to the child, who was barely fourteen. But even so, things settled down. The child grew sisters like growths on her hands. One day she would run up the hill home, and the next day she would appear with a duplicate, perhaps a little smaller and thinner. One by one her little sisters filled the house, appearing magically at mealtimes only. They were part of the mysteries of the house, and Lydia became accustomed to the hungry, wide-faced children.

Benito looked and moved like a man of fifty, and was always in excellent health. La Comadre Matilde said that he was preserved in alcohol. Whatever the reason, he was always steeped in liquor. He drank more in a week than most people in a month. It was almost as though he kept his stock of life in the assorted bottles of fermented cane juice that he kept around him. He had a kind of superstitious fear of running out at any time, so he hid some of the bottles, small flat quarter litres, all over the outhouses and gardens. Wherever Lydia chanced to look she would see one, in the fork of a tree, in the hen house, under a bush, by the side of a drain, all with one last drink in them. Benito's great age, and the security that this army of concealed bottles brought him, gave him an air of serenity.

He would sit on the stone edge of the veranda, or on the long carved bench that had once been in the cathedral at Trujillo but was now in the main corridor of the house. His skin was tawny yellow and his eyes were brown and bleared with drink. He looked very straight ahead, and he teetered rather than walked; and yet, other than an aura of liquor that he carried about with him like eau-de-Cologne, there was no other sign of his alcoholism. His mind and voice were as clear as the pool of water that he had shown her filtering through a wood on top of the hill, filling a basin made by the roots of a huge bucare tree. The new Doña was kind to him, and Don Diego seemed pleased to see him talking to her, night after night. He himself rarely spoke, and Lydia was locked in his silence. She had time for Benito, who was alone with his memories. They were the only secrets and surprises he could offer her.

One night, when Diego had gone early to bed and the house was even stiller than usual, he confided to her: 'You are special, Doña, and different, and very like the people that I shall tell you about. You'll survive when I and all in the valley, and the valley itself, are dead, and it's through you that we won't be forgotten.

'Do you know, Doña, I have given my whole life to the service
of the Beltrán family; and even though they are declining now,
I'm proud of it, and of them. The mountains have always upheld
the old traditions: and the Beltrán family are like a fortress within
the mountains: they are the last survivors. When they fall, I myself
and all of us will fall as well. They are the weathervane of our own
failure. I am their oldest retainer and I've outlived most of them,
and I know more about this valley and its people than anybody else.
Someday the Beltráns may be remembered as tyrants or fools, but
who will see their splendour and their suffering?'

Benito wedged himself into the corner of his seat, intent on
squeezing out his words.

'Who will see how willingly we've all turned on the wheel of
their favour, or how we all strove to stay in the wake of their movement? We used to cling inert to the petrified violence of the hills.
And then we were all swayed by their energy, and their action. The
Beltráns, when they came, rode roughshod through the valley, as
though with a chariot of fire, like meteors. They didn't ride just any
horses, they rode the wild horses that roamed the hills, and they
never quite broke them. On clear nights I can see them bucking
and rearing in the distance. They have all gone now though. Only
the nags are left.'

Benito mulled all these things over in his head, and he brought
them out little by little, unravelling them to La Doña. She was
one of them, though she did not fully know it yet. The sun chariot
would not die, it would rise, thanks to her, in some faraway land.
She would find order in the chaos, and action through his words.
Almost every evening was spent on the veranda: Benito huddled
under his hat, the string fastened tight around his baggy trousers,
his machete by his side, and Lydia Sinclair, the new Doña, with
her hands round her knees, would sit listening beside him. He told
her, 'At first, the tales might seem too gloomy, but under the heavy
canopy of funeral trappings, you will see that it is just that we have

learned to find our strength in death. It lives in our houses. After you, too, have felt somebody's death, you will gain the strength to record our lives. Someone's dying will make you strong.'

The hummingbirds had left the roses and the clematis. The stables where Don Alejandro Beltrán, her father-in-law, had watched the donkeys mating were empty now except for spare pieces of machinery. Jeeps and trucks and lorries in various stages of disrepair were dotted around the grounds in a state of abandon. An avenue of avocado trees stretched out towards the town. A great marble staircase curved up into the night. A long flagged corridor opened out into the inner garden on one side and onto endless dimly-lit rooms on the other, like a lopsided fishbone. Diego took refuge in his bed more and more often now, closing his eyes on everything, closing his eyes too on his wife and his family's lands, as though sleep alone could make all things whole, and stop the decline that he felt beginning to come. In his long siestas, he was gathering strength for a more decisive action, against his withering avocado groves and his blighted cane, and his own swollen kidney that allowed him to sleep like a child and sapped his will and lulled him so easily into inertia.

The cicadas and the grasshoppers sang to them with a tuneless insistence. Napoleon, the vulture, sat close beside Lydia's hammock. His wings were folded behind his back, and he kept his head cocked slightly to one side as he crouched, both attentive and restless, preening the absence of feathers on his scrawny, grey-black neck where the skin sagged in folds. Wrapped in the evening and the sheen of his own plumage, he too knew about kings, and how to keep quiet, and when to attack. But what the vulture knows best of all is to bide his time. Benito used to soothe him, saying, 'Wait, and it shall be yours.'

When the chores of the day were over, when the clothes were sorted and the dogs fed, when tomorrow's corn was soaking in lime, and the beans in water, Lydia would lie back and listen. At first she listened more to the haste of the millrace and the rumbling of the millwheel than to anything else. Then she heard the muffled sounds of the sugar factory; and from the hut on the hill directly behind her house she heard the old man Natividad, who was eighty, and had milked goats and made soft cheese, wheezing with his quarter of a lung, and praying under the clamp shadow of the banana palms for each quarter of a day: Natividad, whose daughter did not love him, Natividad, whose stiffened hands could no longer grip the udder, whose mouth was broken, and whose stringy flesh was scrag.

* * *

Time passed, and Diego planned new ways to irrigate his fields, but the dry banks failed him. He showed Lydia how to renew the crops, but a strange fungus burned them. Lydia planted the garden, and her own dogs dug it up. She fed the stray cats, but the stray dogs killed them. She bound the cracks in her home, and the machete wounds in the cane fields. She learned to lower fevers, and to raise hopes, and she learned to decipher movement in the stillness of the people. She and Diego saw the power wagon, known as La Povva, trundle across the bridge on its last trip. Laden with damaged sugarcane, and held together entirely by chains and scrap metal and ropes, La Povva lurched past them to the mill with men and boys hanging from its sides like flags. Diego had retired to his rooms for four days after that, grieving for the sugarcane.

Two years had passed and the Povva had always been there, swaying to and fro, strange in its camouflage paint, an ex-army lorry waging war on the crumbling roads. Now there was no more cane, no more working mill or wheel, just disused monuments, and La Povva rusting in a field. Natividad, too, was dead now.

For the Christmas of 1955, Don Diego called his sixty-five workers to him, and, dividing the arable lands of his estate into equal lots, he gave one lot of land to the care of each man there, together with a share of his mules and seeds. He had kept a similar lot for himself, and one for Lydia, and he kept most of the unterraced hillslopes. But there was a new tyranny rising in the valley: the drought.

II

With the change of crop and the changing climate, the structure of Lydia's life changed too, even her hammock worked itself loose and began to sink to the ground. She stroked Napoleon, and watched the moon's phases and the vultures rise. Napoleon hardly ever flew: he strutted and hurried in his strange-necked way. He seemed to have no desire to leave her. Even though they sometimes fought, he would remain. In these middle years, in the face of her own marriage's failure, Lydia fought and challenged everything that threatened to erode the valley's strength. In 1956 she acquired a special status and was grafted onto its blood: after three years of infertility she was with child. Even Diego, who practically never spoke now, not to her or to anyone, rallied at the prospect of a child. Their unborn heir sank slowly towards her pelvis and waited, as she herself waited for a pattern to come back to her life.

Meanwhile, she challenged and defended until her teeth ached from the effort. First she summoned her housekeeper:

'Comadre Matilde, why do the corn and beans taste of stale dust?'

La Comadre turned her slow, bovine face to the corridor and said,

'Doña, there are weevils in all the bales and jars. A scum of brittle bodies floats on the soak-water of every pan of beans. It is a sign'.

And she crossed herself.

'Just as the maggots in the cheese are a sign'.

Here she put down the lump of dough that she had been kneading and crossed herself again. Collecting up the huge mass of raw bread she stepped into the corridor, and, opening her eyes wide to give weight to her words, she asked, rhetorically,

'And what about the milk souring no sooner than it leaves the cow?'

Almost reluctantly, she set aside her dough, studded with grey shell-like corpses, and turned to face Lydia, who had followed her. Then, in a voice of constant apology she said,

'Doña, long before Don Diego was born, when Benito was a young man, and I was a child, the sky turned the colour of blood and fell to the ground. There was a thundering like the river crashing down the valley in flood. Before the end of the day, the cloud rose in a continuous sheet. It just rose and left with an even louder whirring. Afterwards, the light returned, but all the land was bare. They had ripped away every tree and stalk and leaf, leaving the valley like a desert fringed with bedraggled banana palms. That was the year of the locust, Doña.'

Lydia was shocked. She had heard of the plague of locusts before, many times, but she was always shocked by the devastation they had caused, so she urged her old housekeeper on.

'What did you do, Comadre? What did you eat?'

'We collected up great mounds of dead locusts, Doña, creatures so strange that they could not be God's creatures.

'They were evil and we scraped them together and burnt them. Then, for nearly a year, we just ate bananas: fibre, juice and skin. Death never took such a good harvest, not even in the years of the black vomit.

'Every time that a scrap of food is wasted, I remember. Every time the young ones say that things are bad, then I remember how bad they can get. And every time I peel and cook the green bananas for your table, I think: the locusts are coming, slowly now.

This time they are eating out the land and the trees. This time we can't see them.'

'But this is different, Comadre.'

'Yes,' said the old woman, turning painfully towards the kitchen once more. 'This time it is different. Now the trees are burning before the plague. The forest fires are taking everything. These are the years of ashes!'

Napoleon kept very close to Lydia, sticking like a plumed growth to her heel. He ignored the other vultures overhead. Each day he became a little more temperamental, and his erratic behaviour began to border on the delinquent. He was even upset with Lydia. His chatter was no longer bright and gentle, he went off his food, and no little sore was safe from him now. He was not content with keeping at bay Calichano, the old man with the rotting leg who came with the corn. He would dart out at any wound, however small, and dig his long, curve-tipped beak in. He could rip through the hide of a cow, and break through a skull. If his mistress left him, even for a moment, he would fly into the kitchen and pull down all the plates from the rack and smash them on the flagstones. One day one of the workers threw a stone at him and broke his leg. Lydia mended the bone as best she could, and plastered and bandaged it. It was the first time that she had ever had to set a leg and the bone didn't knit well. While it mended she had to keep him still, but he would tear through all her ropes and thongs, so, finally, she chained him to the base of a bamboo tree. Napoleon seemed to shrink there, as he sulked and pined.

Meanwhile, Lydia was nearing the time of her lying in. At six months, she felt more than anything else that she wanted to halt the valley's decline before her child was born. From her window she could see the silent mill. There was not enough grass for cattle, and goats would just beat their hooves against the ground like a tom-tom of death. Nothing ever grew where goats had grazed.

Insects ate into the crops, or drought burned them out if they managed to get started. She enlisted the neighbouring peasants and, taking command with renewed vigour, she brought sheep to her dying farm.

Even Don Diego was enthusiastic and ferried the sheep in over the frontier from Colombia to their lands. For the first time in two years the valley shook off its apathy. The workers steered the newly-arrived sheep into makeshift pens. Batch after batch of ewes arrived, bedraggled Romney Marshes that had been shipped halfway round the western hemisphere, packed in with hordes of thin, kicking Afrikaners. Many of them were dead on arrival. The very young and the old had slipped in the lorries and been trampled by the others, dragged down, soaked in urine and soggy droppings. A few of them lived on like that, caked and damp and broken, but they were mostly buried in shallow graves on the edge of a field. Napoleon cocked his head and closed one eye, while with the other one he blinked as though counting the carcasses, and he sharpened his beak. Under their matted coats the sheep were ridged and anaemic. But they began to fill out on the unending hectares of weed and scrub that were all that was left of the Hacienda La Bebella. And despite the volunteer workers thinning out, there were still enough to tend the straying flocks.

The sheep were a moment of respite. They strayed through the overgrown fields like alien beings edging through the beard and nostrils of a giant face. One sneeze could shake them away, yet they remained, and became a part of the land, scoring through it as they grazed. Napoleon moved back from his foul nest by the bamboo where he had let no one clean away his droppings and stale meat, and he resumed his place by his mistress. A stranger came one day asking for advice, and as Lydia stood listening, Napoleon leapt in a rage of jealousy at her sandalled feet, and ripped at one of her bare toes. She saw the pool of blood before she felt any pain, and then the two surged up in anger; and, seizing a brick from the edge of a flower bed, she pursued the offending bird down the avenue and across the bridge and all along the shady path that led to the disused mill of a neighbouring farm some miles away. Her torn foot bled as she ran, but she was aware only of the thick sticky odour, and the blinding sun on her bare head, and a wish for revenge that spurred her on far beyond her strength. By the time the abandoned chimney stack came into view she was exhausted. The bird darted past her and made off towards home again. She turned and followed, noticing now how absurd Napoleon looked, half-running and half-limping with his wings flapping wildly behind him, squawking unintelligibly as he went. Long before she reached her own mill and bridge, she took stock of her own ludicrous position, nine months pregnant as she was, posing as a dishevelled wrath of God, brick in hand, chasing a ridiculous vulture who mocked her by not flying away. She saw Benito staring at her in alarm, and relented, and laughed.

'Curse your eyes, Napoleon!' She called out after the disappearing culprit, and then, to Benito, 'Help me home, will you; and bring coffee grounds and frailejon to stop the blood – that idiot bird has massacred my foot.'

That same night the child was crowned, and Lydia prepared the carved oak cradle that had been in the family for years; the local midwife was called, but she found the delivery a difficult one. She told Don Diego that the umbilical cord had wound itself five times around the baby's foot, and while he was being disentangled he breathed in the amniotic fluid. 'What does that mean?' Diego had asked her dully. 'It means it's bad, señor.' The boy who was born was called Alejandro Beltrán Sinclair. His face had a strange, wax-like beauty, and he seemed restless and cried all through his first night. La Comadre Matilde began to spread the news that the new heir had water in his lungs.

Doña Lydia was exhausted and tearful; she felt the child's death in her veins and she could not bear it. The women from the estate hung around her house, and from her room she could just hear them chattering, and she guessed by the tone of their voices what they were saying. From the kitchen she heard La Comadre crooning to herself:

'Sleep, my little lord, sleep while you are able.
This long night and the moonlight are yours,
But not the morning.
In this land of cradle-cap,
Yours is the fairest cradle.'

La Comadre was always making up songs.

Doña Lydia shut herself in her rooms with the child. Her husband wandered in and out, not quite sure what to do; he paced around for half an hour at a time and then left. By her bed, Lydia piled up soiled plates and clothes, and new ones took their place. For days and days she just watched and held her baby, listening to his breathing for the least sign of improvement. The christening came and went. The child was hurried into the church at Mendoza, the first Beltrán to be christened without a cardinal or even a bishop there. But Lydia was too tired to know or notice.

Napoleon tapped on the mud-mortar of the wall of her room. He wanted her back. His tapping was growing frantic. Each day of the baby's life was a triumph for Lydia, and a source of fury for the outraged vulture.

One day, she dozed in her rocking chair and awoke to see Napoleon's head sticking through the wall. He had opened a hole in the brickwork and his turkey neck was poking through. His skin hung down the wall like an elderly scrotum, and the glint in his eye was evil. He glared at the baby with jealous savagery. Lydia looked up at his grotesque neck framed in plaster, and she knew that he would have to go. That day, the baby's breath came more sharply. His face tightened and seemed to stick in a gasp of pain and then the breath was released in a wheeze of relief. The pattern accelerated until the whole room shook with the tremor of his lungs. She held him up to the sun as though it might be able to ease his pain, but it only showed up even more the paleness of his skin that was turning steadily bluer as his breath failed him. Racked by spasms, the child lost consciousness every time he managed to exhale. His pulse stopped, and his mother breathed for him, kneading his heart and giving him breath. He relaxed a little, and she kept on helping him, and then he stiffened, and still she cradled him. Nobody dared to take his rigid body from her arms. They were locked together and she sang to him in a strange language that no one could understand.

When they finally took the child from her, he would not fit in his little white coffin, but she would not let them break his bones to straighten them, and another, wider box had to be made. She had reached the beginning of the end.

III

Diego Beltrán had always wanted but never had any children; the baby's death left him winded as from a fist in the groin. He drank a lot, and when he was alone he wept, and all the while he worried about his wife, who would let no one near her. Lydia had locked herself upstairs in the library. Her eyes stung and the room swayed, but she could not cry. Exhaustion had dulled her brain. Everything that she had had poured out through the gap that the child's absence made in her arms. She felt a thud on the edge of her consciousness: Diego was knocking at the door of the next room.

'Lydia, let me in.'

Through a missing knot in the woodwork he could just see her, staring out towards the river and the mill. The night would hold her in its chill cramp, and by day she would be much too hot, but she didn't move. Her body seemed not to have or need any natural functions – even her bright hair was tarnished in the sun.

Her friend the doctor came, and spoke to her through the door, and he begged her to weep. Benito hovered outside her rooms, a fixture among the changing visitors. He tugged at the rim of his hat, and he, too, wanted her to weep. The whole valley besought her to weep as they had done – the river could not hold their tears. Their acceptance of death was not callousness: they were like serfs on its lands.

On the third day, Diego broke open the door. She turned her face away but he knelt beside her, reasoning quietly with her:

'We pay tithes,' he said, 'but we are never free. Death is a part-time lodger in all of us. We all differ, but we do have a common denominator: there is no guarantee of survival. Life is more than living here, it is constant war. We cannot win, but if we stick together we can, at least, keep fighting. To avoid disputes as to whom to support and defend, we are moved by what is family. Our loyalties are firstly to our family, and then to our dead.'

He pointed to the women waiting outside the house.

'Every single one of those women has lost a son, if not several.'

Lydia looked up, and towards them, and then slowly away.

'If you think that they cry too readily for our son, whom they never knew, it is because they are crying for their own dead as well as for yours and for you. For most of us there is no horizon further away than the crest of the hill, and we have no refuge other than in each other. We cling together like threads in a cloth, and death is our undoing. We are threadbare, Lydia, and you are one of us. In spurning our help you spurn our grief as well. We try to live a little more, a little better, and in that extra bit are the lives of our dead. It is too hard for them to die and let nothing remain in their stead, so we carry them with us, as added strength. We do this despite the strain, but so many have died that there is always a certain sadness inside us. Whenever someone else dies – and there is always someone – then we come together and share our grief. It is the one time when we allow ourselves to weaken. What hope is there for us all if we cannot see the shadow of our sorrow in the eyes of friends?'

Diego stroked her hair and his voice became more insistent:

'Don't harden towards us, Lydia – life is hard enough already.' He stood up and walked towards the door. When he turned, he found that she was crying to herself. He sat with her for a while, holding her in a relieved silence while she felt the chill leave her bones, and a warm patch like a hot poultice spread over her chest.

After this, when she looked back, Lydia came to feel that there had been a clear succession of catastrophes, accumulating their debris in great dunes that changed the pattern of her life. It was in her sixth year on the estate that the sheep's disease brought a change. They stared as though with stale eyes. They moved stiffly and with difficulty, their joints seeming to crunch. It was hard for her to believe that they were really ill. They lowered their heads and trembled, huddling together in the ruins of Natividad's, the dead goatherd's, hut, and then they began to wheeze. It was this ordered convulsion that distressed her most. It seemed that death itself wheezed through many lungs in a sick cloud of heavy breath from which there was no escape. Ever since her first night on the estate, silence had incorporated the cicadas and wheezing. It was the only rhythm left in the hills. She tried, to the last one, to save her straggling flock, but she knew from her manuals they had anthrax: she could hear the oedema in their tissues, like ground glass under their skin.

They buried the carcasses, and the half-charred remains brought down the vultures. There was such a glut that they picked and chose, and a mass of rotting offal was left.

The fires on the ground were matched by fires in the scrubland on the hill. It was as though the peasants were hurrying towards their end by burning the last few stalks and leaves. Benito told her that it was an old custom of the Timotoquican Indians to burn down the hills as a sacrifice to the sky in times of drought. It was meant to make it rain; in fact, it sealed the drought. Many people died, and many left. Lydia and Diego, Benito and Matilde huddled together. Benito made coffee, and told them about the past. Whenever Don Diego came down, Benito told him anecdotes about his father. They all believed that it would rain, with time, and they were all waiting.

Napoleon was never forgiven for having wanted to savage her baby son. From the day he broke a hole through her bedroom wall, he had ceased to be a pet. All his gentleness had gone. Antonio, the foreman, took him to his hut until something was decided, and he kept him chained there. His wife claimed that he was a bird of ill omen, and, finally, that either she or he must go. The foreman saw that the land had dried out, the river was poisoned and three of his own children dead, so he agreed to get rid of the bird. The next morning he said to Lydia,

'My wife is going to kill the vulture.'

'Don't kill the bird,' she said. 'Give him to someone who is leaving, tied up in a sack, and give the man this corn, from me, to let him loose far away from here.' So saying she fetched the grain from her own dwindling store. She missed Napoleon, as she missed many things; but the Hacienda was still her home – it was where she belonged, and its history had grown under her skin like the anthrax.

The sugar mill became overgrown with weeds, and then bare again as the weeds were burned down by the sun. Diego would go and sit there sometimes. He and Lydia seemed united by some invisible bond, that kept them close to each other, but alone. It seemed that the Hacienda was all that was left of their marriage. They never spoke of it, but they both knew and accepted that Diego had a kind of sleeping sickness of the heart. When their son had died, he had pleaded with Lydia to weep, but now it was she who exhorted him to speak, meeting only his silence by way of an answer. The tall chimney tower and the mill machinery remained like props to the stories that Benito told her. As the years went by, he told her hundreds of stories. Some he repeated more than

KEEPERS OF THE HOUSE

others. For instance, he often spoke of Diego's great-uncle, Arturo Lino, for whom he had worked since they were both boys. He also talked about the dynasty of Don Rodrigos who were descended one from another like Egyptian kings.

Years passed and only their crippled cousin Cristóbal came by, hobbling on his one remaining leg. It was a lonely way to live. Lydia remembered how she had once hidden in the reeds of a little ditch that ran by a ridge of trees, avoiding some particularly irritating visitor. Benito told her that that was exactly where Cristóbal used to hide when he wanted to be alone. She was pleased by the coincidence – it seemed to draw them closer.

More than anything, Lydia buried herself in her research. There was little else to do: the flowers that she used to draw had all dried up. And the beagle hounds that had numbered fourteen and taken up time had gone down with distemper. Only one bitch survived. This bitch had sailed from England ten years before, and time seemed to have forgotten about her. She even thrived on her diet eked out with corn grit and bullet-hard beans. Diego disappeared for a few days and reappeared with a mate for her. The dog was quite unlike his bride in shape and size, but not altogether impossible as a stud. But even he was sick. Ulcers began to form around his oversized penis, and maggots chewed at his sores. Wherever he went he left little red puddles, as he cocked his stubby legs, marking out his new territory, with his haemorrhages. The others wanted to put him down, but Lydia insisted on trying to save him. He was a newcomer, like herself: no one else would help, so she doused the dog with creosote on her own and cauterised the little craters in his flesh. He seemed to recover for six months but the sarcoma was still there; and then he died, wasting away in his last five days of life to rib and spine. She buried him under the avocados, close by, in a plot so full that she housed a veritable cemetery in her garden. For a long time afterwards, the sight of his rotting penis filled her dreams.

Benito and Lydia became a well of mutual strength. By day it was her hair that caught the sunlight, and by night it was his skull that shone as he spoke. Together they kept the house running, under the sad eye of La Comadre Matilde, and the manic isolation of Diego, immersed in his *Lives of Napoleon*, lying more often than not open and over his face while he dozed fitfully in the hammock on the veranda, or in the half-light of his shuttered rooms.

Even those people who earlier had decided to stay on were now leaving the valley. Reports from elsewhere were very bad, but they left all the same. They had faced death for a long time, sacrificing a part of themselves to its yearly harvest. But they could not bring themselves to sit still in the certainty of being swallowed up by the drought and by sickness. It was a strange sickness that defied all cure. It was like a mockery of what the valley used to be: an alternate shrinking and swelling in an abscess of pain. Even with the locusts there had been hope.

Diego saw his people leave, and what was left of his willpower drained away with them. He had a bed made up for him in the library – the same room where his baby son had died years before – and he took to it and turned to the wall. He slept that way for the best part of a year. He would prop himself up to eat and to reach out for his chamber pot. Otherwise, he slept.

La Comadre Matilde left one day and the last they saw of her was her limping shapeless back struggling down the road in a dust cloud. Her cousin and the children had disappeared long before. Benito gathered up stores from abandoned homes and carried them back by the sackful. His booty included a vast supply of moonshine liquor, which he surreptitiously drank, and the two of them sat alone, immune to the sickness, staring out at the hills, and watching for the passage of Cristóbal; and waiting for rain.

IV

Lydia remembered how Benito had said to her:

'You have come from the past, from our past, to witness this family's decay. Fate has brought you here to us, to chronicle our decline. Our history is like the history of a whole country; you have come to save it from the sand. This drought has been the last blow, but our strength had already gone before. You, a foreigner, are our only heir.' Lydia was at a loss to know how to set about such a task. She was not a natural storyteller, in fact, like Diego, she rarely spoke at all. She began by imagining people one by one as shapes on paper, cutting them out and threading them together like beads on a rosary, or stones on a choker. The introduction was a huge face coming over a hill. It seemed that the whole chronicle could be the passage of the sun through the valley. The tale about Arturo Lino, the murderer, she saw as a millstone with a soft shaft in its centre. The two aunts who played cards all day, gambling to decide who should do each chore, were discs divided into segments by thin rays of sunlight. The segments dealt around clockwise, but one overlapped in a backward deal. The massacre of the family was like a stairway with a banister of crossed swords.

There were endless details that she had missed and whose absence puzzled her. Benito could always tell her what she needed to know.

'Benito, why are those iron wheels in the sugar mill always so well oiled and never used?'

The old man would adjust his hat and straighten his machete as he began.

'Don Alejandro, your father-in-law, God bless him, had them brought here when the road was hardly a road. He always wanted to have a really big sugar crusher. He didn't want any of the cane to be wasted, so he bought a huge cane crusher that would extract more juice than any other, but he died before it was ever mounted. His last words were that it was mangling him. Don Diego used to oil those cogwheels himself – they are like part of the family.'

Lydia imagined fire in the furnace, and thought of the different oven doors through which it was stoked. There was the fire of her father-in-law, the dying man who didn't want to die. Then the fire of a barren woman who burned herself out; and the fire of an unsatisfied woman who could not get enough love. Behind them, like furls of smoke from the factory chimney, were her own husband and his uncle Elías who sought but could not find. She saw them as five cogwheels interlocking like stars, with the river as their shaft. There was a touching, but no hold.

Lydia gathered notes and photographs, letters and deeds until she had more material than she could remember. She began to write down all that she was told on loose sheets of paper. After a year, there were so many notes that she was obliged to put them into some kind of order. She decided to begin in the late-eighteenth century with the arrival of the first two Beltráns, and then to continue in chronological order. Since the farm was derelict, she had no work other than to care for her husband and herself and Benito, and to sort out all the chests of photographs and papers. Something from every story ran through her own house. There were letters from Elías in New York, and the telegram announcing his death. There was an X-ray of a face with no jaw. In the garden there was Arturo Lino's millstone. She used to sit on it although she felt that it was still his. There were fat bundles of photographs, snapshots of children. There was even a faded watercolour of cousin Cristóbal and his brothers playing in the shrubbery at her own house. Cristóbal was the oldest. She would write about him last. That would seem right, because he was ageless and would outlive them all. His tale seemed to be lines, like roads, and they must move up and down from town to village, from La Caldera to the *páramo*. There would be no other characters but him and the land. Some people said that she had come to witness their end; but he had witnessed their lives. Cristóbal had rejected his lands and wealth, and his silent presence had prophesied their doom.

Lydia watched him pass, with his usual string of vultures in tow, and she missed Napoleon. She wondered if he were there with the other vultures overhead. Time had ceased to pass in any ordered way: it was just there, and it passed slowly. She was aware of growing older, and she knew that Benito had begun to wheeze. Her hammock was low on the ground now, and its dragging sway filled her eyes with the dry filings that the woodworm left. Looking around, there wasn't much left. She could no longer muster any troops. The electricity had gone and the town was a ghost town. Her house and garden were in ruins. The Hacienda had drawn a full circle of decay, with the difference that she was strong inside it, and thriving like a crab on the dead meat of its neighbours. Their stomachs were swollen from the fullness that was sweeping through the land. Only she was swollen with child. She looked at herself in a cracked glass: she was windswept and sunburnt and strong – fair match, she thought, for disaster, like a bride.

Most of the days were spent sitting on the edge of the chimney's plinth in the disused mill or upstairs with Diego, in his shuttered room, or sorting papers from one room to the next. Diego had become like a sepia print of his ancestors. His silence was like a main joist and his eyes were sad like Napoleon's and, like his, they followed her around. Lydia was shifting the dust and the moths from the study when she heard him bellow, 'Lydia!' and she turned and went to him. She saw that he looked like her father had done the moment before he died, and she knew at once that Diego, too, had had a stroke. She held him as he arched and then went limp, and she knew that the paralysis would stay with him until the day he died. She held his inert hand and, cradling his head, she wept for him and his stillness. Benito was right, she had become the keeper of the house. Later, she found herself weeping for her own inadequacy to bring their centuries' strength into her chronicle. Looking out over hectares of dried weeds she remembered sadly that something always happened on the third stroke of a time signal. She knew that for her, on the third stroke, it would be time to go.

Cristóbal still came and went, with his wound and his staff and his wild hair. She would have liked to have asked him how many more people survived further up the valley. But she feared that there might not be any more; besides which, he never spoke. Cristóbal bore a strong family resemblance. Diego had always liked and respected him, and he would blanch with anger if anyone said he was mad; he used to say, 'Cristóbal isn't mad, he's suffering.' Lydia hoped that Diego wasn't suffering under the screen of his damaged brain. Even though it meant trudging up and down the stairs twenty times a day with what she now sensed was growing inside her, she didn't want to move him. The room had been his choice, and she stuck by it. Parts of his body could still move, but only feebly, and he had grown thinner. Despite her own scanty diet, her womb had stretched to extraordinary proportions by the time she was halfway through her pregnancy.

Benito and she sat very close together in the evenings regaling each other with stories that they both knew off by heart. They filled the corridors with nostalgia, reminiscing about the days when there were eleven working mills in the valley. One night, flying red ants came. They had come before, heralding storms, but that night they descended like a frantic cloud. They came by the hundred thousand in a mesh of wings. At the best of times, they flew into clothes and eyes, up nostrils and into open mouths. However, that night, they were far worse. They concentrated around the inner courtyard where the full moon shone most brightly. Benito and Lydia watched from the darkness of their corridor. Lydia said, 'Listen, their falling bodies and the beating of their wings seem like rain.'

The old man nodded. 'Yes, but it's like the red rain of the locusts. Even real rain could not change all this now.'

Lydia looked towards him in alarm. He caught her eye and struggled to change the subject.

'Doña, what will the child be called when it's born?'

'If it's a boy, he shall be called Rodrigo like the earlier Beltráns, I suppose, or Alejandro. And if it's a girl, well, probably La Bebella – I'm not sure yet what else.' Her words petered out into the night, and she searched quickly for something to say to hold the old man a little longer. But it was time to go to bed. Every morning it was Benito who woke Lydia up, and at the end of the day his last words were always, 'I'll see you in the morning, Doña.' But that night he said,

'Wake me in the morning, Doña; and may God bless you and keep you from harm.'

Then he walked slowly to his room at the back of the house. Hobbling away, without his hat on, he was like a shrivelled dwarf. Lydia's heart went out to him, but she knew that he knew best. So she too went to bed, hardly sleeping, in the knowledge that Benito was not well.

V

The sun had still to climb over the mountain crests, and the mornings were still cold. But the landscape was blackened with burnt woodlands and singed fields. Lydia awoke early and left her husband and his paralysis still asleep. She laboured with her clothes, her every movement was ungainly over the bulge of her pregnancy, but she still wore the Edwardian dresses that she had brought with her, with their dozens of buttons. Before she walked down the marble staircase, she paused to observe the remains of her house.

There was a covering of dry earth everywhere, blown in and steadily drifting around the walls and pillars. The cobwebs over the arches that linked the inner halls had thickened into curtains, and the woodworm and the giant bees had drilled through all the furniture leaving only the old cathedral bench intact. The garden had fared no better. That morning, she missed the grey fluff of cane flowers over the railings, and the carpet of discarded leaves after the harvest. Apart from a few dandelion stalks, solanum and cacti, and herself and the two men, everything was drying up. The door to Benito's room was on the outside of the house, and the room itself was crammed full of oddments. She knocked on his door and called to him. There was no answer, so she went in. He was curled up as though asleep. Lydia picked her way across the piles of chipped and broken china, and the stacks of fragmented tiles, and the bundles of ragged shirts that Benito clung to. And there were sacks of bric-a-brac, and liquor and candlewax and relics. It was only a small room, and she saw that Benito, half-buried under the clutter, lay dead. His hat and machete lay on the floor beside him, and he had dressed himself in the cream jacket and trousers that the moth had mostly eaten, and that were his most treasured *liki-liki*, his ancient best that he had kept as a funeral suit. Lydia had only to sit with his body and then bury him.

There were no flowers for Benito, but she found a few leaves and some dandelion clocks, and even a candle to light at his head. The fluffy seeds blew away and she thought, 'We shall have to go, too.' She sat all day and all night with Benito's body. Before dragging him out to the burial plot under the avocados, she stroked the wrinkled skin of his face. Curled up on his bed, Benito reminded her of a man she had seen in a museum as a child, mummified in hot sand, completely dry and brittle, with two fingers broken off and lying beside him. Benito Mendoza looked just like him except that instead of fingers, there were little bottles of cane liquor under his hand.

The earth was too caked to break into. Try as she might, she could not dig a grave. After an hour's work she had not moved a single spit of earth. She gave up and found a slight dip under another dead avocado tree, and she half-dragged and half-carried him into it. She had all his favourite belongings ready: liquor, hat and sword, machete, a fish hook and a radio, a penknife and a flowered shirt. She also put in a box of unidentifiable objects and some presents from her. Then she scraped up enough dry soil to cover him. He was laid face downwards so that the vulture would not get his eyes, and on top of the earth she put heavy stones for the same purpose. The final effect was like a primitive long barrow. Lydia cried while she buried him, more than she had ever done before. Benito had had a great stock of theories about the right time and place for things to happen, and he believed firmly in the power of the order of events. Lydia knew as she turned to the mound that he would have found her weeping appropriate. She said, as she always did before going to bed:

'I'll see you in the morning.'

Then for the second time she thought, 'We shall all have to go.'

* * *

The next few days found her sitting by the mound, cleaning out the rust and the sand from the engine of the last jeep on the estate. She knew that there was petrol in a deposit in the sugar mill. Time was running out again, as it had in the days of the sheep, and she had to hurry to leave before her child's birth. She kept close to the old man's grave for company, but it was she who did all the talking now, turning over everything that Benito had told her, storing it up for the day when she would write it all down.

I

THE FLOOR OF GOLD

I

EVERY day, Lydia Sinclair would climb the steep slopes behind
her home, and escape from the stifling heat and the flies below.
From there she could survey the valley of the Momboy fading into
the distance, and the crumpled blue of the hills on the horizon, and
the wild sage and the clinging elders beside her. And she could just
make out the bald path along which the first two Beltrán brothers
who came to the Momboy had ridden. Old Benito had told her
the story as they sat in the corridor of the big house, under the
night-flowering jasmine, that gripped like incense and was called
locally 'Lady of the Night'. But it was out on the hill slopes with
the hawks and the buzzards, and a clear view down the valley, that
she best remembered the tale of the two brothers and the floor of
gold that they were to discover.

It was a windy afternoon of late 1785 when the two brothers,
Rodrigo and Sancho Beltrán, appeared on the horizon. They had
been riding for many months before they came to the Hacienda La
Bebella. Far to the south, in their own country, they had plotted
and led an uprising that had been betrayed, and both had been
banished. Their lives had been spared, in consideration of their
eminent and, until then, loyal family, but exile had been inevitable;
and now they roamed these foreign, unfriendly lands, wending
their way north, hugging the foothills of the Andes, whose terrain,
at least, was like the country that they had left. They crossed the
frontier at Cucuta, and they had been riding for some hundred and
fifty miles through what seemed to them to be a vast, neglected

estate, following the course of a widening river, and observing their surroundings with some surprise.

They travelled on horseback, with a train of mules in tow, laden with provisions of food, ammunition, tinder and goods to barter. The river, that they had followed so keenly, was the Momboy, rising on a bleak windy plain in that cold part of the Andes known as the *páramo*. The short, stunted grass that covered the less-exposed slopes became almost imperceptibly a swamp, a trickle and then a stream that swallowed up icy pool after pool as it gathered force, feeding a wealth of woodlands on either side; until it reached the humid unhealthy town of La Caldera where it flowed reluctantly into the much larger river of that name, and was lost in the backswirl of its waters. The Momboy seemed to resent being swallowed up so, and it would retaliate, flooding time and time again the miserable homesteads that were witness to its disappearance as it struggled to turn round.

The two brothers viewed its progress, much as Lydia did, nearly two hundred years later, watching its banks stretch out on either side in varying greens. There was the pale yellow green of the banana palms, stunted by the wind, giving shade to the shining dark green of coffee plants. The brothers hacked and picked their way through the overgrown path that twisted along the deep red carpet of decades of unpicked berries that softened brown every year and then became a black slime under the great sticky mess of palm trees that fell under their own weight. For as far as they could see, the land was overrun with weeds. Crouching under the layers of petticoats that these weeds made were scattered the meagre homesteads of the local peasants. Each night the brothers would stop and exchange news with them, just as they had done in all the months previously. However, they could learn no news from the sullen silence of these men who showed no desire to barter, or even to rob them.

Both of the brothers were struck by the sense of doom in the valley; and although they had witnessed much poverty in their travels, they had never before seen such despair. No one showed any interest in their buttons, and saddles and cloth; there were only blank stares huddled around smoky fires. The peasants were hungry, with a dull hunger that ate into their guts, while the strange fermented liquor that they drank soaked through their bodies and destroyed them like a wasp in their bowels. Weeds overran the clearing that they made, choking the Indian corn and the beans. All their tools had long since rusted and fallen apart, and with only their bare hands they scraped together the sticks and twigs from around their homes to make fires, and they took refuge in their isolated homes from the onslaughts of the climate and disease. They drank their lethal, acid liquor and chewed the grey, mildewed grain.

Whenever the two brothers arrived, they were given wooden cups of hot, muddy coffee that was always faintly mouldy from the rotten beans it came from. The peasants stared in silence at the two intruders, who were, in turn, moved by the generosity of these people who had obviously survived for generations, numbed by hardship and half-starved. The brothers watched how they would retreat into their crumbling huts, and squat amid the piles of damaged food, warming their slight bones over the fire that held them huddled around its flames. They were awaiting death together, burning the lice and giving birth, festering and multiplying almost against their will, concentrating their scant energies in sticking together no matter what, and keeping their fires alight.

High on the hills, safe away from the flooding river, life became a slow panic to survive, centred around tending the fire and spitting stale, recycled saliva that had once held tobacco, and sheltering from the cold months of rain and the chill damp mornings of every day. Ill-fed and in rags, they were no match for the biting wind; it took them up and scattered them, prising open their heads. The two brothers unburdened a half of their mule train, giving food and woollen cloaks and knives to these men who had become like wild creatures of the hills, and who, in their abject poverty, did not know that they were, like themselves, heirs of the conquistadores. Although they spent their lives staring into their rotten-wood fires and looking for sticks to burn, their forefathers had come to those same lands following the de Labastidas in their search for the gold of El Dorado. Their only vision of gold now was the gold of the flames, and the two brothers left them to their red-eyed wheezing, and rode away down the valley to the gates of a ruined mansion.

The brothers were filled with strange feelings as they wound their way to the great house that they had seen in the distance. They wondered what kind of family would live in such a grand place while surrounded by so much neglect. They wondered, too, what sort of a welcome they would receive – since they planned to ask for shelter. Stopping in peasants' hovels and palaces alike, with their fine clothes growing threadbare, and their horses growing thin, they were a far cry from their ancestor, Laurado Beltrán, who had travelled to Spain in 1209 in the train of the German Princess Sabia. They felt a desolately long way even from their family's estates in the far south of the continent.

It was the thick, sweet fragrance of night jasmine that roused them, long before they reached the house itself. They paused to take in its fullness, and to examine the buildings they were approaching a little more closely.

Rodrigo, the elder of the two brothers, was struck by the thought that it smelt like home: half of his own childhood had been spent under the cloying scent of the white star of this night jasmine that had been his mother's favourite flower. Now, looking down the valley, the brothers could see a crumbling mansion almost concealed by a tangle of high weeds and climbing plants. As they drew nearer, they could see the skeletons of unburied horses behind the stables, and the rubble of what must have once been a high wall surrounded the house and its numerous outbuildings.

On one side, there were the remains of an orchard, degenerated now into a dozen immense guava trees towering over the dried-up trunks of almonds, oranges and medlars. On the other side was the house itself, flanked by pillared corridors, while the walls were studded with dozens of low bay windows, these last covered by wrought-iron bars trellised with thick-wooded roses. The whole house seemed lifeless, but for two figures, barely visible in the alcove of one window. Disconcerted by what they had seen, but not deterred, the brothers advanced very slowly, with their arms at the ready. Until they were in hailing distance of the house they feared an ambush by bandits, but when they recognised the sex of the two imprisoned figures, they became at once intrigued and reassured.

II

The twin sisters who sat behind the barred window, cloistered in the half-light of their cluttered drawing room, had stayed that way for over twenty years, since their early childhood. They stared out over the tangled roses and clematis at their vast dowry of lands. Nothing ever moved, except for spiders as they cleaned out their webs, or ants trekking to and from their nests; and yet, that evening something seemed to move out on the skyline. Neither of the sisters could remember anyone ever coming to their house, and they could not believe that the two horsemen silhouetted against the sky could really be riding towards them. The strange intruders were coming down like half-gods from the hills, and the moonlight caught in their fair hair like haloes of pale fire. Nobody was allowed to visit their house, no visitor was welcome, and yet the two horsemen came pressing on, seemingly unaware that the whole house was taboo to outsiders.

The two brothers, Rodrigo and Diego Beltrán, the horsemen, did not know that these twin sisters were the only heirs of the de

Labastidas' family fortunes. Alone in their drawing room, they were nearly suffocated by spoils and overflowing trinkets, trunks full of moth-eaten heirlooms: brocade and needlepoint, lace, and bale upon bale of finest silks now lined these trunks in fistfuls of powdery mess. The brothers did not know that behind the façade, and the carved-wood pillars that reached right up to the roof, supporting a whole string of balconies, the house itself was crumbling away, drilled through as it was by woodworm and beetles outside, and chewed by cockroaches within. The only sound room left was the drawing room where the two sisters sat, on the threadbare tapestry of the window seat, looking out at the hummingbirds that teased their prison bars.

The family of the Marquis de Labastida, of whom these sisters were the last survivors, had first come to South America on the third voyage of Christopher Columbus in 1527. The Marquis's son later joined an expedition to the interior of Venezuela to seek the gold of El Dorado in 1547; and it was this son who had settled in the valley of the Momboy, and been granted the bulk of all the lands around him by Royal deed. However, this son was so proud that he believed not only that none of the native women was good enough for him, but that no one, whatever her title, nationality or wealth, was eligible unless she was actually a full member of his own distinguished and noble family in Spain.

Thus, he remained a bachelor until his old age, when two of his first cousins were finally shipped out: one, to marry the now doddering old millionaire, and the other, to keep her sister company. The one who was to marry her half-blind cousin was called the child Bebella, and all of her husband's estates were renamed in her honour. Despite the honours and the welcome that they received, the girls knew that they had been sent like sacrificial victims, offerings to their family's name and fortunes; they had come to vegetate and become yet another layer of the deep rich humus. Plagued by insects and snakes, the child Bebella bore a son to her husband who had, in his turn, crawled over her like a pale reptile feeling its blind way home. Her child married her nephew, and so began a long tradition of intermarriage: cousin to cousin, and cousin to cousin, until the name of de Labastida, which had nearly become extinct, multiplied itself like a banner of repeated syllables trailing behind every decrepit member of that inbred family.

By the time that the Beltrán brothers arrived, de Labastida had become synonymous with a whole string of faults and failures: spindly legs and weak hearts, premature deaths and uneven features, half-witted laughter, and, most characteristically of all, grey staring eyes with half a blue pupil clearly demarcated. The last two de Labastida sisters had also been brought up in the family tradition within the confines of their walled garden, and they had gathered the last nectarines and medlars. They had had no one but their servants to play with, or even to talk to, since their father had gone prematurely senile. He kept them locked in like two captive princesses, while he himself contrived a way of taking his dream of El Dorado and his hoards of gold with him when he died. He knew that his family would die out, now that no one was left to marry his twin daughters. In his more lucid moments, he was astonished by their height and beauty; but even so, he would ensure that they never married: for over two hundred years the family had intermarried. Now that there were only these two twin girls left, he determined that they should die childless, preferring his name and his lands, his wealth and his superb manners should all be lost rather than break with tradition. He himself had always been prepared to die for his honour and the purity of his blood. The least that his daughters could do was to suffer spinsterhood for their lineage.

The old Marquis knew that the long siege was coming to an end: already the garden walls were caving in; his estates would fall from decay; and people from the village would come and pick over his belongings. He felt that they would trample his daughters' needlework, and rub their greasy hands on his silver chalices; lie with coarse blackened feet on his linen sheets, cover their mules with his Persian tapestries, spit tobacco on his marble floors, and tread cow dung into the porcelain tiles; they would defile his property and appropriate his wealth, but he was determined that they should not have his gold. Let them inherit the tangle of weeds that spread for hundreds of thousands of hectares across the hills; let them blister their hands cutting back the undergrowth in search of the scant berries from his coffee plants; but they would not have his easy wealth – not his gold!

So, stealthily, night after night in his house of lethargy, he had raised up the floor tiles of his once splendid hall, and buried a little heap of gold under every tile, until one of the largest fortunes in the country was hidden under the hand-painted ceramics of his floor. His daughters, who were used to hearing strange noises as the house strained and collapsed at night, never suspected the hidden wealth that they walked upon; and they didn't know why their father gloated so, on his deathbed.

Until the Beltrán brothers rode over the hills towards them, the twins spent their time shifting pots and pans to catch the leaks in the roof; being fed by their arthritic servants on gnawed grain, soured wine, and the stringy remains of sick hens; and nursing and humouring their father through his last years of life. As the old man lay dying, his mind wandered and then returned, time and time again, to extracting promises from his daughters. He made them promise never to leave his estates, and never to marry any of their neighbours or countrymen, no matter what. He made them swear this twofold oath on their bibles and on their rosaries, by all that they held sacred, and by the memory of their dead mother.

The twins watched their father dying, and they relinquished all the hopes that they had ever had of marrying and escaping from the decay of their massive homestead: they were doomed to remain among their ruined treasures. Their father took a long time to die, and, in his last months, he struggled with the paralysis that held down half his body and centuries later would seize his last descendant, and he wept for the fate of his two lovely daughters, but he refused to raise his ban. His sick room stank, even to him; no pomander or sal volatile could change it. His room had become a hovel, and he, a wreck; but he smiled as he died, to think that with all his ruin, his precious gold was safe.

His two daughters buried him, and wore mourning, and they prayed for his soul as they told their rosaries in the alcove of the gothic window of their chapel. Gazing out across their abandoned lands, they resigned themselves to growing old, and they heard the vultures overhead laugh at their spinsterhood, and they saw the bleached bones of the unburied horses crumbling under their eyes, and they stared towards the horizon, for want of anything better to do with their lives. And that night of late 1785, they saw the Beltrán brothers standing outlined against the moonlight, and then come riding slowly towards their house; and they called to their ageing maid to come and see whether their eyes deceived them, or whether someone really was coming up to the gates of their prison.

Over the top of the thick knotted stems that covered the lower part of their window, and through the thinly peeling bark of the guava trees, they could just see the path that led up to their house. The Beltrán brothers, who had already caught sight of the women, holstered their pistols and drew closer to the veranda. Then the elder and the taller of the two, Rodrigo, dismounted and tethered his horse, while the younger one lingered behind, covering him in case of trouble. He rang the great cast-iron bell, listening to its echo rebounding off the cavernous walls of the stairwell. The twins straightened their caps and their dresses, frantically trying to invent some menu that they could offer the travellers for their supper, but the food stores were so damaged and scant that there was no help but to endure their usual thin soup and sour wine. Outside the door, the brothers listened to the uneven shuffle of the lame servant who was coming to answer their call. Once inside, they laid down their swords on a lopsided table in the hall, and then went in to present themselves to the de Labastida twins who were shortly to become their wives.

For the two women, swaddled in their spinsterhood, the arrival of these two men – whose presence and place of origin defied their father's ban – was the solution to all their troubles. The brothers stayed on at the Hacienda La Bebella, lodged in the ramshackle wings of the old house. They brought in labourers from the hills, and livestock from the village, and day by day they brought more life to the dying hacienda. They began to salvage all that they could from the old house, and with the help of local labour they built a new one. Much of the original material could be seen there: noticeably, the marble columns and stairs, and the stained glass from the chapel. However, they added wooden pillars to the verandas, carved out of whole cedar trunks, and every window led out onto a balcony, so that the old feeling of imprisonment should never be felt in the house, and every room should be open instead of closed; and they called it 'La Casa de Balcón'. Then they carefully transplanted the night-scented jasmine, and its dark leaves and simple starry flowers began to climb up new walls. The last part of their work was to prise up each porcelain tile from the shell of the old house, and re-lay them in their new hall.

They had no idea that the thin layer of tiles concealed a deep bed of gold pieces. Square by square, they unearthed the hidden treasure: never in their lives had they seen such hoards of it, not even in the viceroy's coffers. They were especially careful not to break the tiles that covered their trove, and they attributed to them great symbolic importance, since it was the beauty of the tiles with their animal and insect motifs that had led them to the discovery of the concealed gold. Chest after chest was filled with it, until all the chests were full, and then all the sacks and bags that could be found were filled to bursting and then stitched and tied.

At the time of the uncovering, there were dozens of local people working on the new house and on the grounds and in the fields and, in their minds they confused the floor of gold with the Beltrán brothers themselves. And it was even believed that the heaps of treasure that some of them had seen miraculously appear on the floor of the old house were woven extensions of the Beltrán's hair, which had often struck them as being a blend of gold and the sun itself. And the peasants grew as fond of these fairytales as they were of their new prosperity, and of the Beltráns themselves.

The two brothers buried some of their trove in a special pit, built for that purpose, and some of it was spent on luxuries, but most of it was spent, over the years, on innovations. New kinds of grain and breeds of cattle were imported. And the three towering sets of stables could boast the finest horses from Ireland, France and southern Spain. Andalusian donkeys and packs of mules were ferried from La Guaira to the Andes, and master craftsmen came from the Canaries and the colonies, and followed the long route with them, over four hundred miles of cobbles to the Momboy. And new trees were shipped in bales of wet hay, and nectarines, pomegranates, walnuts and almonds. In the garden, there was all that the old Marquis had once had and more, while inside, the carvers and plasterers, glaziers and masons all laboured to turn La Casa de Balcón into a veritable temple.

Much later, the Hacienda La Bebella still rejoiced in this renewed splendour. Until well into the twentieth century, it would have the finest farm equipment, livestock and installations. And just as many of the Beltráns would devote their leisure to inventions and improvements that they would send out and patent and use themselves, they kept a keen eye open for other people's discoveries. And thus, they brought the first bicycle to the country, owned the first sewing machine in the state, and the first wire recorder, and the first pianola. And in 1934, they brought the first motor car to its roads.

One day, General Mario Beltrán would be their best-known inventor. In the very early days of electric light, the Hacienda had its own dynamo, fed by the River Momboy, that could light the big house or the sugar mill by the turn of a lever. And the electric plant of the town of La Caldera was drawn up by General Mario, who would also devise a new way of making sugar, and build a hospital, and die a leper.

But long before any of these things would happen, the first two Beltráns were building their new house, and they took pride in its every detail, from the bales of silk for the counterpanes of the eleven bedrooms, to the stocking of the library. Despite the fact that every book had to be carried the four hundred miles by mule back, they managed to represent every author of any stature, past and present, from Aristotle to Swift, and from Gongora to Racine.

In less than a year from the time of their arrival the Beltráns had married the twin sisters, and they were both well contented with their respective brides. The older brother, Rodrigo, and his wife, Rosa de Labastida, stayed on the estate, and founded the Beltrán dynasty that was to rule the valley for nearly two hundred years. Their heirs were to stay with the land until the land became a desert, and the last Beltrán was Lydia Sinclair's unborn child. Sancho, the younger brother, took a share of the gold and a mule train of provisions, and set out for the distant town of Coro with his bride.

III

The first Don Rodrigo set aside a special room in which he stacked his sacks and chests of gold on the one side, and the glazed and patterned ceramic tiles on the other. With time, the room became a second chapel in the house, and the carved-ivory altar grew as the sacks receded. After his death, many an heir would sit in the dimly-lit and heavy atmosphere of this little chapel poring over the tiles that had covered the mythical floor of gold. Each tile seemed to hold a piece of their history, and they would upturn them, like fragments of a puzzle, and then lay them down again, the wiser for having glimpsed into the past.

Many years later, as the tiles became chipped and broken, they were gradually discarded, and they lay scattered in the fields and gardens. The oxen dragging their ploughs would churn them up and then bury them again. Children playing would scratch up the coloured chips and throw them in the river, where they lay on the riverbed like jewels. Even later still, these vestigial chips of Moorish art were collected and placed in huge bowls and jars, and treasured in playrooms and nurseries, by the children whose forefathers had thrown them away. There was no longer any vision of gold in the valley of the Momboy, and El Dorado itself had long since been banished from their thoughts. Yet something of this dream had rubbed into the scraps of broken porcelain that had once hidden centuries of wealth, and they were worshipped on secret altars where they sat like a pot-pourri of events.

By the time that Diego, the penultimate Beltrán, was born in 1920, the stacks of tiles had been reduced to a mound of a mere twenty. He memorised all the tales that their family and servants, and the peasants who came down from the hills, told him; and when he knew that he would not be interrupted, he would creep into the storeroom where the tiles were kept, and turning them over in his hands he would repeat the tales. In the loneliness of the midday siesta, Diego found it comforting to chant the lives of his dead ancestors. Just as, during the famine of the year of the locust, his father had soothed himself by stroking and whispering to the same tiles, and his grandfather, the last Rodrigo, had cooled himself on their glaze, treasuring them as Catholic relics; and his own wife, Lydia, held them in her solitude. When Lydia left the deserted valley of the Momboy, she took one of the tiles with her, to keep for their unborn child. Looking back, it seemed an odd thing to have done, but at the time, it was only natural that she should take a part of the most powerful object on the hacienda: the floor of gold that had caused their rise and witnessed their decline.

The best time for being with the mound of tiles was always in the afternoon, between the hours of two and five, in the time known as the 'dead hours'. This was the time when, on the parched slopes of the Momboy valley, the air was most oppressive. It was a time too hot to do anything but lie still, in comfort – even the mosquitoes slowed down their whirring to a lazy hum, and the dogs lay flat out with their bellies stretched across the stone floor.

Diego found solace in handling the glazed clay, shuffling the brittle squares like so many cards, dealing them out like patches to cover the empty places in his life. The tiles sat like a series of cold poultices on his loneliness, in the half-light, through the dead hours, together with old letters, and later, photographs, gathering first mould, and then dust.

Diego would sit through the dead hours of each day, reliving the past through their presence. Each tile was like a specific time or incident in his family's history. Most of the incidents were within living memory of the old men on the hacienda, and he, Diego, had heard them told time and time again in that special way that mixed both fact and fantasy. It was a way of speaking that swerved from the truth only in quantity: numbers were increased and multiplied in a constant effort to compete with the vastness of the elements shaping their everyday lives.

There was little time or energy on the hacienda, after the drudgery was done, for anything other than tales and talk; and everywhere there was the underlying wish to rise above the hardship of floods and tremors, to plant a mark on that country that kept each of them slave to the ravages of disease. This wish to excel showed itself in everyone's speech: no one felt hungry, they felt starving; they were never tired, but dropping; not full, but bursting; not worried, but distraught. Likewise, there was never a mound of washing, but a mountain; any number over ten became thousands; the slightest defect became a monstrosity; and each kind word or gesture was inflated into raptures of virtue. For the local people who toiled from six until six every day from early childhood to death, the coming of the Beltráns to their valley was a fulfilment of their wildest fantasies, since their very presence and their every deed were extremes in themselves. The people championed the Beltráns' strength, and wallowed in their eccentricities; and, best of all, they loved to retell that family's history to such willing listeners as young Diego Beltrán.

Alone, in the windowless room where the tiles were kept, Diego would remember all the stories that he had been told and it seemed that he could read the details from the different patterns of the old glazed squares, like an archive with page after page of deaths and entries. On one tile he could see his grandfather, the last Rodrigo, with a platinum jaw, and a piece of his left ear shot away, and the tile told him of the duel that his grandfather had had with Diego's great-great-uncle Don Juan, when he had lost that piece of his ear, and had never spoken to his uncle again, and had even written into his will that his grave should lie at some distance from that of Don Juan, so as not to be plagued by his presence after his death. Diego had heard that Juan had challenged his nephew to a duel, and that they had both gone, in private, to the bare ground behind the clocktower of the stable block, and that Juan had fired the first shot, but his hand had trembled, and the bullet had merely whisked off his nephew's ear, while the last Rodrigo, who was the best shot in the country, had thrown down his gun and walked away, with the blood drenching his shirt, because he knew that no aimed shot of his could miss its target, so he walked away, rather than kill his young uncle – but he never forgave him. Nobody ever knew what the two had first quarrelled about – they were both hardly more than boys at the time. In the evenings, when Diego's grandfather had sat out on his veranda, throwing gold coins in the air, and shooting holes in them, many a curious bystander had tried to learn the cause of his duel and feud, but no one ever succeeded. True to his wish, the two men were buried on opposite sides of the graveyard.

Some of the tiles were just broken chips, with the hint of half-told stories, such as the Beltrán's kinship to Bolívar, the Libertador, through the de Labastidas and the Briceños and the Caxels and the Sanmaniegos Cuaresma de Melos. It was the litany of names as much as the links themselves that the Beltráns loved. Bolívar's mother had gone from the Andes, taking with her the glory of the future Libertador, who would be the first President, and founder of a new Republic, but her name remained, in the family archives. And, despite their loyalty, their energies were devoted to those who stayed. So their cousinship to Cipriano Castro, one of their most feared dictators, passed almost unnoticed, while less historically significant figures were often remembered merely for their foolishness or pride.

Occasionally someone would overreach himself in these two spheres. One such man, in particular, was Leoncio Beltán. Leoncio was, by all accounts, an excessively proud man, much more akin to his degenerate de Labastida ancestors than to the rest of his family. He took unusual pride in his dress and appearance, he spoke to very few people, and he liked to remind all and sundry that his was the noblest family in the land. From his early boyhood he regretted being born when he was, in 1862, long after the titles of the old Spanish court had been abolished. By way of revenge, and to make quite sure that everyone knew that it was his family who had settled there, he always insisted on using fourteen surnames in an exaggeration of the old Andean custom of using two and sometimes four. By the time that he had got as far as Don Leoncio Beltrán Carvajal Beltrán Briceño de Labastida de La Caxel de León de Labastida... very few people had the patience to hear him to the end, and this little piece of snobbery was unpopular, not to mention cumbersome. One tile remained to show how, on one occasion, it had stood Leoncio in bad stead. He had gone hunting one early morning in the upper valley and, by the descent of a sudden mist, he had become separated from the rest of his party. Devoid of any natural sense of direction, he had roamed the hills, straying farther and farther away from his horse and men. He had walked for some ten miles across the wet bracken and wild sage of the hills, and it was cold and windy. He had no food or blanket with him, and as night fell he realised that he must find a homestead and ask for lodging for the night.

The mere thought of asking for anything was torture to him, but he felt that there was no other choice, so he trekked on until he saw one faint light in the distance. He walked up to the one small wooden house that he saw and knocked on the door. An old woman came and, opening a tiny grid, asked his business. He told her his three first names and his fourteen surnames, and said that he had lost his way in the mist, and had come to ask for lodgings. To which the old woman replied that had he been on his own she would have gladly put him up, but since he came with the great string of men whom he had mentioned, she hadn't enough room or food for such a troop, and had slammed the grid shut on his aristocratic nose. He could not bring himself to knock again and tell her that the 'great string of men' was just his cold, tired self, so he went and spent the night on the open slopes, cursing both his own folly and the biting wind.

The glazed coverings of the floor of gold, and the tall men on their horses, and the memories of the old men, were all that Lydia needed to begin to retrace the chronicle. Diego collected the broken chips and splinters that he found in the fields and in his garden, and he treasured them all, like a child, in the dark room; and later, when he lay paralysed in bed, he kept what was left of them beside him, and he fingered them with his hand that moved, remembering not only what Benito and the others knew, but also what his father had told him, about those few Beltráns who had left and then returned.

There was one in particular, called 'Admiral Silence', who had entered the civil service and become so successful that he was promoted to customs-officer-in-charge of the port of Puerto Cabello on the hot coastal plains far away from his home. He had gone, and stayed in the lifeless tropical town for twenty years. Finding nobody with a spirit akin to his own, this once vivacious member of their family had executed his job in total silence, writing notes and memoranda to his subordinates, and choosing to have no social life at all. His one concession was to go every evening at exactly seven o'clock to a steaming bar, where he always ordered five glasses of whisky, one after the other. This he did by shaping his thumb and forefinger to the height of a small whisky glass, and holding it up to the bartender.

He made none of the grunts and mumblings of other mutes, but rather carried himself in such an imposing way that he was respected and left to himself by all the town, who referred to him as 'Admiral Silence' because of his connections with the sea. Only one man ever came near to him, and he was an engineer who felt irresistibly drawn towards this silent figure in the bar. Every evening for twenty years, he would go and sit at the same table as him, also drinking five glasses of whisky, which, out of deference, he ordered in the same silent way. No word was ever exchanged by the two, the engineer not daring to speak, and Admiral Silence not wishing to.

However, one evening a freak storm hit the town, threatening to flood it entirely. The rain was so heavy that roofs were caving in, people in the streets were being hammered against the walls of houses, barely able to hold their ground. In the midst of this storm, the engineer came gasping into the bar, where he remained for some time regaining his breath. He drank a first glass of whisky and then went and sat at his usual table. On looking out of the window, that was keeping only a third of the rain from leaking onto their table, he wiped his streaming brow, and commented,

'What a storm!'

Whereupon Admiral Silence drew himself up to his full height, and his pale face quivered with irritation as he replied, speaking for the first and only time in twenty years,

'Did you come here to drink, or to gossip about the weather?'

Diego felt a brotherhood of silence with this curious ancestor whom he had never known.

IV

Sometimes, when Diego was a child, he had smuggled a little stock of tiles outside, and he would sit with them somewhere to get a slightly different view of what he saw in them, in the different light. His favourite place was always the dank brick surround of the huge waterwheel that stood to one side of the cane crusher. Anyone could come in and disturb him inside the big house, once the creaking of hammocks had stopped, and the household were up and about, but behind the giant wheel in the sugar mill he could sit for hours with the precious tiles. He didn't know why, but whenever he sat thus, behind the wheel, his mind turned to disease.

Perhaps it was because, in one form or another, it was always present, hanging like a falling canopy over their lives. He knew that the local people saw his family as a saving force that would see them through their constant battle with disease. Old Benito Mendoza used to say that the Massacre of the Beltrán family in 1903 had been the turning point in their history, and the first of many steps in their slow decline, but he, Diego, saw the first sign of ill omen in the prolonged disease of his great-great-uncle, the military hero and inventor, General Mario Beltrán, who died of leprosy, after twenty-three years of suffering and shame.

Before this event, his family and the valley had survived through marauding bands and earthquakes, through droughts and floods, through fevers and epidemics, and each time the trouble had passed, and they had recovered their strength. Smallpox and the black vomit, typhoid and diphtheria had all come and gone, leaving a trail of new graves in the cemeteries and a sense of loss in their homes; and each time, it was the Beltráns who rallied first, swallowing their grief and gathering their strength like wrestlers ready for the next round.

Yet, in the 1870s, when a strain of leprosy came buried in fresh cheeses brought down from the hills, over five hundred people were contaminated before the cause of the epidemic was found. Most of the victims died that same year, often of secondary illnesses, but the disease wormed its way into the body of General Mario Beltrán, taking that one man to be the living memory of its passing.

Diego looked more closely into General Mario's tile, and in the cracked glaze of its surface he saw the features of a man in his mid-thirties, alone in a large room, hidden behind a mask and gloves and shielded by a screen. Nobody but his wife knew of the gradual disfigurement of this once handsome man. Not even his servants knew that each year his fingers were shrinking and falling away as his hands turned to unwieldy stumps. He allowed himself no children; and no man ever came close to him again. He spoke like an oracle from behind his screen, and his house was full of mystery and secrecy.

General Mario felt the sickness in his blood like a curse. In the afternoons, behind a long table, sitting in his creosoted wooden chair, touching nothing without his gloves, so that nothing should be infected by his leper's touch, catching his breath whenever footsteps neared, so that not even his breathing should contaminate the air, he would look out across his gardens and draw up the many sheets of plans for a new system for producing sugar. From the day that he first diagnosed his illness – already well advanced in its trek through his limbs – to the day he died, he never set foot outside. Through the French windows he could feel the breeze teasing the numb regions above his bandages. He would have liked to go outside, but he felt that even his tread was contagious, and he would never infect the land that was dearer to him than his own life, so he remained in solitary confinement.

For over twenty years he pencilled his graphs and diagrams, as he watched the erosion of his flesh, and the stumps of his hands were the hillsides. He watched his mutilated bones lying in the valley of his lap; incurable, but stubborn as he struggled to control a pen and compass in his deformed fingers. Although the disease plundered his life, he would never give in; death would come one day to end his torture, but until then, he would stand witness to his ruin. From behind his screen, he laid down the law: every object that he touched must be burnt, and his plates be made of clay, and smashed after one usage; no one should ever approach him, and no one comfort him – not even his wife.

The local people became more and more intrigued by his mystery, and would walk or ride for days on end in order to ask his advice, or for him to settle some dispute. They used him like an oracle, and were drawn to him for reasons that they themselves never understood: his very presence seemed to calm the anxiety of others. Everybody knew that he was untouchable, but no one realised why. They had glorified the military victories of his youth and they had honoured him the more for his being a national hero. Details of his battles and campaigns were remembered with pride. No one except for his nephew, Rodrigo, really knew what he was doing with all his papers – it was whispered that he was planning one last campaign. In fact, he was designing a new wing for the town's hospital, based on the findings of Florence Nightingale. During his twenty years inside his screened sickroom, General

Mario kept his decay a secret. He filled his shelves with improvements and inventions but his prophecies with gloom, and his words were full of warnings.

He defied his leprosy, and died of a heart attack, like most other men in his family. His body was sewn into layer after layer of thick sacking, and his coffin lid was nailed down at once, in accordance with his own orders. He had also commanded that no one must come into the room of his wake, but that all mourners must stay out on the veranda, and that no one should see his face. And there was no mass said at his funeral, except for the very shortest obligatory prayer, because he had said that he had foreseen in frequent dreams the fate of their valley, and no thanks were owed to any God who would ruin such brave men.

II

THE MASSACRE

I

THE land known as the 'Beltrán country' stretched for some hundred and twenty miles along the River Momboy, fanning out on either side over hills and more valleys. To Benito, it had always been the Beltrán country. By the turn of the century, of all the haciendas that covered the land, Rodrigo Beltrán's was the busiest: he and his lands combined to form the heart of the valley. He was one of the many heirs of his namesake, the first Don Rodrigo, who had reached the Hacienda like a stranger, and died there like a saint. And now, over a hundred years later, everything that this latter-day Rodrigo said and did merely added to his already huge reputation. He was a symbolic hero in the flesh, an uncrowned king and leader of his people. Five of his brothers farmed their own neighbouring estates, while the sixth, Arturo Lino, was locked away in a madhouse.

Rodrigo's cousins on his mother's side, the Briceños, were jealous of his popularity and power. Lydia knew that there had been much rivalry between the two families – mostly on the part of the Briceños. However, the feud seemed to have been healed over when Don Rodrigo married the eldest Briceño girl, thus reuniting the two families. Nevertheless, the girl's elder brothers had still, secretly, been as envious as ever; and one of the younger sisters, María Candelaria, was jealous that her sister should have made a better match than she could ever hope to do.

Benito liked telling Lydia about these times the best. All the anecdotes and tales were about times that he himself could remember, and about people that he had known. His very own brother had helped shape history, and Benito was grateful to Lydia for wanting to know.

'Anyway,' he used to say, 'all those earlier Beltráns who fought battles and won medals and led campaigns and founded towns are all remembered in books and plaques. But the last Don Rodrigo, and Alejandro his son, and my old master, Arturo Lino, are only remembered in our minds.'

These last were the men who had fought the drought and the dust, and the locusts, and their last battle at the Alto de Escuque. But the historians had turned their eyes to Maracaibo and the rise of oil, and no one had looked over their shoulders to the Andes, where the last of the families of the first conquistadores were in their decline.

*   *   *

During the six years after his marriage, Don Rodrigo managed his estates and many of the town's affairs, and his fame as a born leader grew side by side with his reputation as a womaniser. Meanwhile, the Briceño brothers felt their jealousy cut into them like a powerful acid, and there was seemingly nothing that they could do about it.

It was onto this undercurrent of pent-up rivalry that General Polidoro Africano was grafted in 1903. Commander of the Fifth Army, and the youngest full general in the history of his country, he looked resplendent as he rode into the town of La Caldera on a white stallion with silver trappings, dressed himself in full regalia. No man had ever seemed more handsome than he, with his staff and troops marching behind him in such numbers that they disappeared into the skyline and were lost from sight. The General came with direct orders from the President of the Republic to 'placate the rebellious States of the Andes'.

As he rode through the main square, past the rearing statue of Bolívar, he was struck by the sight of María Candelaria Briceño walking there, chaperoned, on her way home from Mass. She had the loveliest eyes he had ever seen, and a pallor that equalled only his own mother's. The young General bowed to her, a stiff bow that showed none of the attraction he felt. She was wild and vain and delighted by the flattery of her new suitor. When she reached her home, her brothers were well pleased to hear that the General had stopped to look at her. Only their mother, Doña Ignacia, was worried by what she heard. María Candelaria was her favourite daughter – there were many others, but it was this one who was spoilt and could do as she pleased. She had been a spiteful, bullying child, and now, at the age of eighteen, she tormented all the young men in the town, waving her beauty before them and then whisking it away. She flirted so much that her mother feared that one day she would disgrace them all.

María Candelaria was definitely not like the other daughters: the girl seemed to need a constant outside stimulus to keep her from being spiteful and bad-tempered; and she was bored with life. The mother knew that her other children and their cousins called her daughter 'María-Llama', because she was like a jet of flame, with her quick temper and withering taunts. María Candelaria was like a bad omen that her mother loved: Doña Ignacia was well aware of the fact that the girl was too lovely, and too light-headed; she knew that her daughter could only bring trouble to her house, yet she held her close, like a cancer in her flesh.

At best, the girl would dance herself to death; at worst, she would disgrace her family. Her mother did all she could to protect her daughter's frailty and frivolity, and to treat her cruelty as though it were an illness that kindness would cure. Neither her mother, nor anybody else in her family, had any idea that she had already broken the rules of their society. The first rule was that all girls should be virgins when they married, on pain of death. María

Candelaria kept her secret and hoped for the best: so far, she had always been lucky.

General Polidoro Africano rode on through the town, guiding his troops towards the army headquarters and their barracks which were some miles outside the town itself, high on a hill at a place called El Alto de Escuque. He thought that it appeared to be a peaceful place: he, at least, had been offered no resistance; and he felt that he could allow himself to spend a little time there, planning his campaign. However, while he billeted out the troops his mind was busy remembering the girl he had just seen in the Plaza Bolívar. That night, he left his officers to themselves, signed a few orders, received some invitations, dined alone in his own quarters, and retired early. He was determined to find a strategy to get to know this girl who filled his thoughts. Even his daily letter to his mother was filled with his new-found passion. He wrote:

Dearest Mamma,

Thanks be to God, we have arrived safely in the town of La Caldera. Very few soldiers were lost on the way, and the few that were went by sickness or desertion. Except for my officers, all these men seem to care for nothing but show; they do not realise that they have been press-ganged to fight. I shall keep them here at the barracks for at least two weeks, without which time I fear for the outcome of my Andean campaign. The townspeople cheered our arrival, and I looked uncommonly fine, you will be glad to hear.

I already love this town because it houses the most beautiful girl in the world. I have seen an angel. She has the clearest, most honest eyes that I have ever seen. She is all innocence, and I shall not rest until I marry her. She alone is the only person worthy to be your daughter-in-law. Now your son has two campaigns here in the Andes. If only you were here, all would be well. Alas, you are not, but we are always together, and I am as ever,

Your affectionate son,

POLIDORO

He sealed the letter, carefully dipping his signet into the red wax, and summoning his aide-de-camp he handed him the packet and gave him his instructions:

'Give notice that tomorrow evening there is to be a ball, and every household of any standing is requested to attend, on pain of my displeasure. And,' he boomed, pursing his mouth into a thin line, 'it is to be an excellent ball!'

The young General had a way of talking that was so authoritative that it seemed to accomplish things before they were even begun. He eased his boots off, and his jacket, and lay down to rest in the manner of so many of his fellow military men. Sleeping out in tents on his foreign campaigns, fully dressed for battle, since he was a boy, had given him mixed feelings about a well-made bed. It felt far too vulnerable without his clothes.

He was pleased with the idea of a ball; that way, he was sure to see the girl again. She was well-born and was bound to be there. He decided to approach her very carefully when the time came, and even thought out the exact words that he would use to address her, but his thoughts were a jumble of backache and tiredness, combined with the startling pallor of the girl's face and her clear grey eyes that had set him alight. From under his exhaustion, he whispered,

'Dear God, make me worthy of her purity.'

II

María Candelaria was brushing her hair, admiring herself in her ebony-framed mirror as she did so. All afternoon she had heard nothing but talk of the young General, and praise for his person. She brushed her hair with petulant strokes – it was so long that she could sit on it, and she never had the patience to brush it enough; it was always splendid anyway, whether she brushed it or not. It was not unlike her everyday life, when everyone admired her, whether she was nice or not. Catching her own eye in the glass, she gazed and then turned away, bored even by her own loveliness. The whole town lay at her feet, but she was bored by it, and bored by her invariable success. She would never choose a husband from among its ranks. All the girls seemed to marry, just to become mere chattels to bear children. It was sickening, but it was what they had been brought up to want. Not she! She wanted grandeur and amusement, and dance upon dance until her head would be filled at least with exhaustion. None of the men in the valley could contain any novelty, nor carry the glory she wanted. She wanted unheard-of fame, fame that would stretch from sea to sea. She ran the brush savagely through her hair, thinking:

'What more do they want of me? I'm not a charity that I should humour their nonsense. I don't even like them. They make me sick! Let them humour me, since they are so bewitched. I need humouring.'

The following evening found her in a similar position, brushing her hair for the ball. Beside her on her chair was the dress that she was to wear. From downstairs she heard the muffled voices filtering up through the floor boards. Her other sisters were in a fluster: one wanted her sash retying; another, a wisp of hair straightening; and yet another had scuffed her dancing shoes. Their hurry was useless, as she alone knew, because they could not leave without her, and she was determined to arrive late. Besides which, how could they hope to shine while she was to be there? She knew how unfair it must seem to them that she should be so vain, and with such reason; but then, she too suffered and was bored and bothered by others. She pinched her maid for being slow, and then again for crying. When she was finally ready, she crossed her fingers and went down, touching her crucifix at every tread of the stair, and wishing herself luck for this one and only chance of ever getting out of the valley.

On the other side of the marble landing her two elder brothers were dressing in their respective rooms. They were both tall and good-looking, and they took great care in combing and twirling their moustaches and buttoning their spats. They knew that their cousin, Don Rodrigo Beltrán, was not going to attend the ball and they wanted to make the most of this unique opportunity of appearing to be the centre of the town. Everyone else at the ball would know that they were just 'the Briceño brothers', but the General and his staff might easily believe that their place in the town's hierarchy was higher than it really was. When they were both ready, they admired each other, and when their eyes met they seemed to say,

'If only the General would propose to María Candelaria!'

They had already worked out the amount of time that the General was likely to stay in the town: it could be long enough to fall in love with their sister, but not long enough to hear all the gossip about her unbalanced behaviour and her perennial flirting. They went and waited in the downstairs hall, taking a keen interest in their sisters' apparel: the whole family must look its best. As usual, María Candelaria was late.

The entire family was restless when she finally came down; standing under the huge vaulted arches of her home, surrounded by centuries of wealth, she mourned the lack of glitter. She would have liked to have turned in a sea of tinsel. 'Let everything be new,' she thought, 'like the General, who at twenty-four has swept the whole country off its feet.'

The man in question, Polidoro Africano, had no idea that the girl he had glimpsed in the square and fallen in love with was thinking of him as she stepped into her carriage. Nor did he know that at every bump of the road, which was not really designed for carriages but for mules and solitary riders, she longed to see him. He took unusual pains with his dress that night. His batman had brushed his clothes three times at least, and his moustache was perfectly curled. He made his way to the ball well satisfied with his appearance but anxious as to the girl's feelings. He was short of time. In two weeks at the outside he would have to take his troops into the hills and crush the uprising that was causing so much alarm in the capital. If anything was to happen, he must be engaged by then, marry on his return, and then take his bride with him on his way back. It seemed an impossible plan, but he had no other; so he thought about it as his horse picked its way over the treacherous path that led from the barracks to the town centre, and the great hall where the ball was to be. His troops were all stationed on the outskirts, in the village that had grown up around the military post. Escuque was a high, chill village, swamped in mountain mists. The path to the town wound round the rock face, leaving a gaping precipice on one side. Towards the end, he hurried a little: he didn't want the girl to arrive before him.

In the dimly-lit hallway he crossed himself and then strode into the ballroom, dazzled by the mirrored chandeliers, and straining his eyes to see his future bride. She wasn't there – she might even be married, he thought; but he was somehow sure that she wasn't. He would wait. He sat down and refused to open the ball. He was taciturn and forbidding – nobody dared approach him. On the one side there was a low hum of disconcerted chatter, and silence on the other. The minutes dragged by, and the townsmen began to fear some kind of trap. During the War of Independence hundreds of people had been murdered at such a ball by order of General Boves, a famous tyrant. They fanned each other and smiled,

'That was nearly ninety years ago; why should such things be feared now? The General looks enchanting...'

'And what eyes!'

'... He isn't wearing a wedding ring.'

'Perhaps he's waiting for somebody.'

'He only arrived yesterday – he doesn't know anybody yet.'

'Isn't Don Rodrigo coming?'

'He said nobody ordered him around on his own property. But that for the sake of peace he would allow some members of his family to attend.'

'I hope that the General doesn't notice and take offence.'

'Well, I know for a fact that María Candelaria is coming; she said that she wouldn't miss it for anything. She'll make us all look dull when she arrives, so we may as well take advantage of these few moments before she does.'

The young girl who had just spoken blushed and turned away, catching sight of María Candelaria as she did so. A hush fell on the ballroom as the Briceño family entered. The General stepped forward, and María Candelaria caught up the roomful of admiring eyes and threw them down like so many pebbles; then, tossing back her head so that her own eyes and tiara would show to their best advantage, she curtsied to the General's bow. Names had been exchanged, they had been introduced, the rest seemed like plain sailing to them both. Polidoro Africano made a sign to the orchestra, and the music began, the ball was opened, and María Candelaria and he led the dance. Her two elder brothers could hardly believe their luck; a match between the General and their sister would greatly improve their own position in society.

By the next morning the town was in a commotion. The two had danced together all night. Even the many women who felt some reserve at María Candelaria's callousness were delighted by the unreality of the match. It was like a memory from a book of fairy tales actually happening in their town. The old women wiped the sweat from their foreheads and, straining themselves out of their many years of heat and hard work, they retold their rosaries with added enthusiasm, realising that they were going to witness a great event. The children stopped squabbling and began to speculate on the time and place of the wedding. All the young girls began to supervise the lace and trimming of the clothes they would wear. The seamstresses' fingers were full of jabs and tears, as they worked overtime before any announcement had even been made.

María Candelaria basked in her new-found glory, until the engagement was announced. Surrounded by the flowers and cards that arrived in her name four times a day, escorted by any number of well-groomed officers, she kept thinking that there was something she had to tell Polidoro. Exactly two weeks after they first met, General Polidoro Africano announced his engagement to María Candelaria, second daughter of Don Manuel Briceño Beltrán. The wedding was to be on the seventh of October of the same year, 1903. The date was chosen because it allowed him time to finish his campaign and return; and also because it was his mother's birthday.

Polidoro was anxious that his wife-to-be and his mother should get on well. They would all live together, and he dearly wanted them both to be happy with him. He had already sent an escort to bring his mother to La Caldera and he had arranged – by exerting just a little pressure – for her to rent a fine house opposite St Peter's Church, near the main square. He knew that she would have time to get to know her future daughter-in-law and all the family too. He had written to her about his engagement with some fears as to how she would receive the news. She wanted so much for him. She must have heard, as he himself had, of the many Generals Beltrán in their country's history, and indeed of the archbishops and governors, vice-presidents and field marshals, all bound up with the history of María Candelaria's family. She was directly descended from the first noble families to settle in the country, even from the Libertador himself – surely his mother would be satisfied! But most of all he knew that she would be appeased if she came and saw with what honours his fiancée's family was treated for hundreds of miles around, and how the eldest sister was married to the greatest man in that part of the Andes. Not even he, a full general, could gain such undivided loyalty as Don Rodrigo could. So he wrote to her:

Dearest Mamma,

I know that six months is almost too short a period for an engagement, but the furtherance of my career requires my presence in the capital as soon as this campaign is over. I beg, therefore, that you come and arrange such details of the wedding and the dowry as must be attended to in my absence. Also, it would give me pleasure to know you to be nearer to me while I am fighting in the mountains. Help me in my hour of trouble, and come to my side.

A house and servants await you, but bring your own maid.

I remain,

Your affectionate son,

POLIDORO

* * *

The troops left for the high mountains with a clatter of hooves and rattling of cannon carts over the stony path. His men were well equipped with boots and blankets against the cold. Many of them were new recruits who didn't know how cold and hard a night on the hills could be, with nothing but slops of hot gruel in their stomachs, and an icy wind working its way into the marrow of their bones. They didn't know the pains that came with exhaustion, like sharp wounds, down their shins and spines. In their bright uniforms, carrying flasks full of rum and fresh water, they mostly had no idea that war was more the days before and after than the actual battle.

They would have to drink foul water from old ponds, and then their bowels would writhe, month after month, in the grip of gastritis and dysentery. In the squalor of their diarrhoea they would find neither peace nor glory. None the less, they set off with a drummer and a piper to march the hundred miles of winding road and track to the stronghold of the rebels. They were soldiers in a country that had been at peace for nearly a century, and they were not prepared for the barrage of hardships that they were to meet: they were parade-ground soldiers.

Their marching was perfect as they went down into the town and then swerved round and out, through Don Rodrigo's estates; and then on through all the Beltrán country for over a hundred miles, until they reached the state boundary. The old and young alike lined the Camino Real to wave and cheer the troops. The greatest cheer was for General Polidoro – at times it was almost a chant:

'Viva Polidoro, vi-va-Pol-i-do-ro, vi-va-Pol-i-do-ro!'

By the end of the morning even the echo of their marching was out of earshot, and the great mass of the rearguard was out of sight.

Three weeks later, the vultures left the town and flew away in the direction that the troops had taken. For several weeks any animal that died by the roadside or in a garden was left to rot, and the heavy smell of neglected death filled the air. Some said that it was a bad omen, others covered their noses and ignored it, hiring people to haul away the untended carcasses. By August the vultures had returned to the town, where they continued to pick stray bones and eat the offending flesh. The wedding date was getting nearer, and the hubbub of preparations took up everybody's time.

It was also in early August that General Polidoro's mother arrived. Her carriage was followed by a great procession of mules and carts. Everyone wondered at her elegance – no one had ever come all the way from the capital in a carriage. They didn't know that only the first and last legs of her journey had been in such style. The rest of the way she had had to ride side-saddle, day after day, till she felt that not a bone in her body was in the right place, so rattled around was she. She settled herself in her new house and made herself as sociable as possible to the neighbours, who grew genuinely fond of this ageing woman who could speak of no one but her only son.

Since no theme was at that time dearer to their own hearts, they learned as much as they could about him: his likes and dislikes, his exploits and honours, feats and medals, until he already seemed almost like one of the family. However, there was always an 'almost', and until he had children and had settled with them, there always would be.

Halfway through September, the troops returned. News of their coming arrived before them, and banners and flares were set up along their route. They returned in tatters, not so much wounded as broken; and there was a glint of repressed hysteria in many an eye. They no longer seemed content merely to pivot around their general's splendour. They had grown restless; but they didn't want to rest, they wanted blood. Cooped up in their barracks again, in the windy village, they brooded on the outcome of their campaign. Although they were told that they had won, they knew that they had lost their pride and sense of being, and the harsh reality of the mountain slopes had frost-bitten their hopes. They told each other,

'Thank God, at least, that the General's wedding will be soon.'

It would cause a diversion in the smother of their disappointment. They waited for the wedding as though to would be their salvation.

María Candelaria was waiting too, but almost reluctantly; she had grown drawn and thin and anxious. She disguised her feelings as best she could, but all was not well with her. She would have to tell Polidoro her secret soon, and she felt the passing of the hours

and days like a scythe striking closer and closer to her. She wanted
so much to live, and yet she knew for sure that she would die very
soon if she did not speak out. Every cell in her body was burning up
in her anguish. It was two weeks to her wedding day, then thirteen,
then twelve days. The mere sight of the preparations made her sick.
There was something that she had to tell Polidoro, and her time
was running out. She knew that if she waited until after she was
married, it would be too late. If she spoke out after the wedding
the fault would be her own, and she would die. She absolutely had
to tell Polidoro the truth about herself before she married. It was
hardly more than a week to the wedding when she told him. She
had forced her mother to leave her alone with her fiancé. And it was
when she insisted that her mother first knew that something was
very wrong. 'You have five minutes,' she had told her daughter, 'and
no more.' But María Candelaria wasn't even listening. She pushed
past her into the sala and then said, very quickly,

'Polidoro, I am no longer pure.'

At first, he seemed not to hear her, then the colour drained away
from his face and returned in waves of pain and anger.

'What do you mean?' he asked between clenched teeth.

'I am not a virgin,' she said.

He felt that his honour was being ridiculed. Pushing and tumbling, he found his way to the street. Behind him, María Candelaria
was weeping,

'It wasn't my fault, it wasn't my fault, I can explain.'

He took refuge in a brothel, where he sat and drank for two
days. He passed out over his table and was carried home by his
fellow officers. Nobody knew what had happened – he didn't really
know himself; he just knew that he loved María Candelaria, and
that someone had wronged her, and him, and his own mamma.
He went back to her house, and demanded to see her alone. She
went into him, trembling, like a sacrificial victim in the hands of
his wrath. But when he shook her, it was not to hurt her, but merely

to make her tell him who it had been. She would not answer, and he shook her even more, screaming at her,

'Whom are you protecting? Whom are you trying to shield? Tell me his name! Who was it?'

She was too terrified to speak and there was nothing but a silent squeak in her throat; but she kept on trying, her arms hurting from his grip; and then she sobbed the first name that came into her head, that could possibly convince him,

'It was Don Rodrigo.'

Polidoro pushed her away and then walked out: her own brother-in-law had raped her. Now he would not marry her until the man was dead.

He called her two elder brothers and told them what he knew. They hated Don Rodrigo and all the Beltráns, who had ruled the valley for too long. They begrudged him his excellence, and envied him his success. Now he had gone too far: here was their chance to combine their vendetta with that family's general downfall. They were ripe for hating, and ready to fight; however, they would take no risks. The General wanted a duel to the death with Don Rodrigo, but that did not suit their plans enough. They wanted to wipe out the whole family, and they finally managed to goad the General into consenting to an ambush.

III

Rodrigo Beltrán was sitting on the veranda of his house, on the last day of September 1903, holding his baby son Alejandro in his lap. That was the way that he spent many evenings. He had two sons, but the elder, Elías, always trailed behind his mother, while Alejandro came and played with him. From where he was sitting he could look out across his estates and at the river that bit its way through his lands. That afternoon he was reflecting on the state of the valley, and the part that he played in its life. He felt that he was as much a symbol as anything else, and wondered if all would have been the same if he had been small and weak. He suspected that it would have made little difference to his followers, although it would have to his enemies.

Tension was mounting around him: he knew for a fact that his brothers-in-law, the Briceños, hated him. They were jealous of everything he did: jealous of his power and even of his success with the ladies. It was true that his reputation in that respect was not unfounded. But it was also true that he loved his wife, their sister, and made her happy while he was at home, and played with his children for hours on end. What he did outside, he felt, was his own business. He wondered what the Briceño brothers would say if they could see him now, bouncing his child on one knee, and a wooden model of a sugar mill on the other.

To the four figures riding down towards Rodrigo Beltrán's house, all seemed as they had expected. They stopped at the bend in the drive and pulled out their watches. It was two minutes to four o'clock. They saw Don Rodrigo through the haze of guava trees, playing with his child, and they waited, knowing that at four o'clock sharp his wife would take the child from his lap. His wife, Doña Juana Isidra, came out of the house and took his son from his arms; the baby didn't want to go and cried out for his model mill. She stooped to pick it up, and then went back again. Don Rodrigo turned to remonstrate, and then he saw the four men who had come to kill him, his brothers-in-law and his wife's two cousins. Cursing, he reached to pick up his gun, remembering too late that it was unloaded. He never played with Alejandro with his loaded pistol in its holster. As he turned back to the house, for cover, a volley of bullets from the elder Briceño's gun hit him full in the face. His hands rose involuntarily to his wounds, but one of his cheeks was gone. The four men rode away while Doña Juana Isidra rushed out holding her terrified children close to her. Trailing behind the assassins, she saw her husband lurching and writhing in his own blood. He turned once to her, and she saw an accusation in what was left of his face. Dragging himself like the remains of some dismembered animal, every part of his silenced body shouted,

'Betrayal!'

She stayed like a stone statue in the doorway, the two boys clawing at her, and it was their screams that echoed down the valley. Doña Juana Isidra just stared at the heap of torn, bubbling flesh that was the man she loved. She had not betrayed him: she had merely saved her sons. Her brothers had told her, two hours before, that she could lose her husband and children, or just her husband. They were going to kill him anyway so they had given her no choice. They had the army behind them, and she knew that Rodrigo would die – was it a crime to save his sons?

They had blown one side of him almost away: half his head and a shattered arm. She knew from the extent of his wounds that he would die: these were his death throes. Rodrigo floundered round the bend and out of sight; even with his wounds and the loss of blood, his prodigious strength held out.

He kept on crawling until he collapsed, spluttering and jawless, with a great clot of blood down his exposed throat. It was one of his workers, the goatherd Natividad, who found him. He was cutting fodder when he heard Don Rodrigo gasping for breath. He went to him, and seeing a man dying of his wounds, he helped him because he, too, had always had a hard time breathing. He put his hand down Rodrigo's throat and removed the offending clot. It was black and thick, and he threw it out. Then he loosened the man's upright collar and was about to leave, when he saw that it was no other than his own master and friend. Untethering his mule, he loaded Rodrigo onto it and rode him into town. He took him straight to the surgeon's house and stayed to help hold him down.

The surgeon worked for hours on Don Rodrigo's wounds. He thought at first that the man was sure to die, and then he gradually realised that he was fighting to stay alive. He sent news of the outrage all around La Caldera; however, his messenger said that the town was nearly empty, and those who were there were heading for the barracks. It seemed that the troops and the Briceños had taken the Beltráns prisoner. Old women stood at the street corners, shouting,

'To the barracks! They are killing the Beltráns!'

Once the truth was known and had sunk in, the local people rallied to their aid, setting off in a great procession along the rocky path to Escuque. Benito was there, too, with the contingent that arrived later, having further to come from the hills. He had often bared for Lydia the grey wound in his shin where a stray bullet had caught him. And he used to say with a tinge of envy, 'Natividad, the goatherd, was there, you know. With him.'

Natividad had seen the surgeon fight his own battle to save Don Rodrigo's life. He staunched the blood and stitched the raw edges, and set his shattered arm in plaster and splints, but there was nothing he could do for the missing jaw and half a check that were blown away. He wondered if his patient would thank him later for having helped him to survive in his new grotesque form. The doctor stayed by Rodrigo: whether he lived or died, he would not spend his last hours alone. He lit a candle for him and placed it on the small altar that he kept in the hall. He knew that Don Rodrigo was an atheist, like most of the Beltrán men; and yet he felt that God could not help but be moved by this bruised and swollen man whose strength could not be broken even at the hour of his death. It was growing dark, and the doctor felt an unfamiliar heaviness in the air. Something unpleasant had settled all over the town. It had never been there before: it had been a violent but an honest town; and even more than honesty, there had been honour. Now, lost with the flesh and bones of Don Rodrigo's face, the townspeople had lost their dignity, and there was treachery in the air.

IV

When the Briceño brothers and their men rode out of Don Rodrigo's homestead, they joined up with the General and his men. Then the General's soldiers began to round up all the Beltrán men and boys, and they herded them towards the barracks, leading them out along the rocky winding road out of town. In one house they found, as the Briceños had said they would, Don Rodrigo's five brothers, their sons and cousins, and his sister Delia, gathered for a family dinner. The General and his men entered on the pretext of taking some refreshment, and then overcame them by sheer numbers: they had all been tricked, taken from behind, and arrested.

While preparations were being made to march the prisoners to the barracks, Doña Delia, the sister, insisted that she would go with them. General Polidoro would not hear of it, since the Briceño brothers' plan was to have his men push all the Beltráns over the edge of the precipice on the way to the barracks, and have done with the whole family. But he had not reckoned upon her stubbornness: she ordered her horse to be saddled, and, bunching up her skirts, rode alongside the General, engaging him in light conversation the whole way.

Polidoro was not prepared for this social chatter. He had not had the stomach to be present at the murder of Don Rodrigo; even though the children had not been shot, it had all been in front of the wife. It had been the Briceño brothers who had wanted to kill him. He himself was very particular about ladies being present. He knew that if this woman, Doña Delia, came along with them, he would not be able to give the order to have the Beltráns thrown over the cliff. She was a serious obstacle, and he must persuade her to turn back.

'Doña Delia, please return to the town. I shall send an escort, and in ten minutes you could be safely home. This is no journey for a lady.'

'My dear General, please don't worry about me; I am positively enjoying the ride.'

'But Madam, this is no place for a lady; besides which, it is quite shocking that you should be out alone at night.'

'As you see, General, I am not alone; I am in the company of yourself, an honourable man.'

The General blushed, and then continued,

'My troops are restless, Doña. I cannot guarantee what they might do in their wildness. I repeat, this is no place for you.'

By now he was thoroughly angered by this one woman who was spoiling his plans. His voice had thundered out his last statement in a way that would have made most men tremble, yet Doña Delia didn't flinch; she just gathered in her trailing skirts a little more, and edged herself even closer to her brothers who were being marched on foot along the muddy track; and, beaming up at the General, she said,

'Dear General Polidoro, how modest you are! It does my heart good to hear you say that you, their supreme commander, cannot control your troops. But then, you always were a gentle man, and it is the honour and number of your victories that announce your power, not your own boasting. Why, all of us know that it is not for nothing that you are the youngest general in the entire army. I know,' she said pointedly, 'that nothing will be done tonight without your orders. I trust you, General Polidoro, because you are a gentleman, and I know that with your consent nothing will happen that either I or your mother should not see; and without your consent nothing at all can happen, General; so, you see, I have nothing to fear.'

Polidoro looked at the woman: short of forcing her back there was nothing he could do. He wished that she hadn't brought his mother into the business. He rode on, looking at her with loathing for protecting the very house that had wronged his bride-to-be.

The procession continued up the stony track; there was only room to move two abreast, so they made very slow progress. Sandwiched into the middle of two battalions, the Beltráns were in surprisingly high spirits. They were approaching the worst bend in the road, where at the best of times it was difficult to pass the narrow ledge without stumbling into the ravine that gaped below. They knew that their arrest was a pretext for their murder, and they knew that no court in the country could try them fairly and convict them of any offence. They had a long history of loyalty and distinguished military service – in the last fifty years alone, there had been two generals, two bishops, three foreign ambassadors and a senator in the family, not to mention the dictator, of whom they were less proud. They knew, too, that they were being led to their slaughter and that the next bend in the road would be the best place to kill them.

The Briceño brothers rode back to where the General was, and the elder of the two whispered to him to send Doña Delia away before they reached the ravine.

'She won't go back,' he said, 'I've already tried to persuade her.'

'Then leave her here,' they said. But the General wouldn't do that: he knew that stragglers from among his troops would mistreat a woman on her own on the road at night. This woman was a friend of his mother's, and now, whether he liked it or not, he felt obliged to escort her to the barracks.

'We shall march to the barracks.'

'But we were going to do it here…'

'I said we shall march to the barracks, and that is that.'

All was not well with the Briceños' plan. They rode on at the head of the troops, but they were beginning to feel uneasy about the outcome of the whole enterprise: the village of Escuque would be as loyal to the Beltráns as was the actual town. However, it was too late to go back; they would just have to take them to the barracks and shoot them there. For as far as they could see behind them, there was a sweeping tail of clattering soldiers; and their noise drowned that of the hundreds of men and women who came hurrying from the town, all armed with anything from pistols to stones, and all ready to fight for the Beltráns. The news was spreading over the whole valley that Don Rodrigo had been murdered and all his family were being taken to their slaughter.

Even before they reached the barracks and its village, the five biggest households who lived there were loading their guns and arming their retainers. Against so many troops they didn't know quite what they could do, but they were determined to do something, so they waited at the ready. When the Beltráns finally arrived, they were crowded into a walled quadrangle, while a firing squad was organised, and Doña Delia escorted to the house of a cousin. She protested, but it was now too late for any more of her delaying tactics to work. There was already blood in the air, and a feeling of violence.

The little village was bracing itself, and streams of outraged people were flocking in from the town. While the soldiers all concentrated around the walled square, the townspeople turned surprise to their advantage and seized the most strategic posts and towers around the square, waiting for the first shot to be fired. The civilians, almost to a man, supported the Beltráns. Even most of the Briceño cousins, who all carried a mixture of Beltrán blood, which gave them the choice of joining either side, did. It was argued that all the Beltráns – apart from Arturo Lino – had behaved well and honourably to the valley, while the Briceños had now used treachery, and that they could not forgive. For centuries they had survived and flourished in near total isolation: with their own laws and their own code of behaviour, their forms of address and speech; their customs and traditions were ritualised because that held them together. More venerated than any saint were honour, loyalty, valour and death. Never before had anyone dared to challenge the Beltráns' leadership of the valley, and never before had anyone challenged the very principles of all of their ways of life. Thus, almost without exception, the people were for the Beltráns.

Inside the walls, some fifty members of the family, a third of them children, were herded together. They had one rifle between them, that Pedro Beltrán, one of Rodrigo's younger brothers, had managed to get by knocking out a guard. They knew that very soon they would be called out through a narrow gate into another yard and that there they would be shot. Whoever went out first, they felt, could surprise their captors and start a fairer fight. All five of the Beltrán brothers and their cousin, Juan, were disputing hotly the right to go out first. The children watched, wide-eyed, and rejoicing secretly when the one rifle passed from the hands of their respective father or favourite into the hands of another. They knew that whoever went out first was bound to be killed and they were frightened for their parents.

Finally, they heard the General's voice calling out for the first five to come through. Pedro seized the rifle and motioned all the men to follow him and take as many firearms as they could once they were in the second yard. He leapt out, aiming his rifle at the elder Briceño brother. His bullet crossed with another that hit him full in the head. Both he and the elder Briceño fell at the same time. The other Beltráns followed, and, taking advantage of the few seconds between emerging from behind the wall and anyone's realising what had happened, they disarmed several astonished soldiers and then ducked back behind the cover of the wall where they had been before.

Those two first shots resounded through the streets of the mountain village, heralding a wave of violence. The townspeople moved into action, picking off the mass of soldiers who were caught unawares against the barracks wall. Some thirty civilians climbed over the wall into the quadrangle where, despite their inferior numbers, they and the Beltráns managed to hold off the brunt of the troops. Most of the casualties inside the quadrangle were from blind bullets ricocheting off the bricks. However, they were too few to be able to fight off the oncoming troops for long; and one after another the prisoners and their supporters were hit and fell. And their ammunition was running out.

There was a constant shuffle of reloading, in which the elder children helped. As Juan Beltrán, Rodrigo's uncle, paused to reload, he looked around and saw a group of frightened children huddling up against the wall behind him, half of them scarcely more than babies. He smiled to them, and shouted encouragingly,

'Never mind, boys, all we need is a couple of miracles and we'll be all right – who knows, we might have another earthquake yet!'

The boys were cheered and relieved, more by his voice than by what he said. As he resumed his post, he put a fistful of cartridges into an empty pocket: there were hardly any left. He knew that soon all their guns would be empty, and then he would rather shoot the children himself than have them murdered by the troops. His own grandsons were there among them; he had seen his favourite, Albertico, not a moment ago, sitting forlornly propped against the wall, holding the hand of another child, already dead. The prisoners' courtyard was littered with their own casualties, young and old sprawled out where they had fallen, the cobbles on the ground and the bricks in the wall were all splashed and splattered with blood. Lower down on the wall, marking their various heights like nursery charts were the finger marks where the younger ones had groped for comfort as they died, clutching at the damp bricks.

Meanwhile, in the main square of the barracks, the townspeople had managed to fight their way in. Most of the fighting was concentrating on one side. On the other, General Polidoro and his aide-de-camp were standing, wondering at the loyalty of the townspeople towards the very family that he, the General, had been led to believe were hated tyrants. They were both heaping curses on the heads of the two dead Briceños who had got them into this riot in the first place; and in the heat of the moment neither of them saw the ragged peasant who was rushing at them. The man was Benito's elder brother. Armed with a machete which he held in both hands, he attacked General Polidoro, slashing him several times along his right side, from chest to thigh, before being killed himself by the General's aide.

A group of officers carried their commander into the low hut directly behind him – it was the map room – and they laid him on a long table strewn with maps of the area that he had covered on his last campaign. A medical orderly was brought to him right away, but found the General already too far gone for any of his skill to save him. It was all he could do to hold back the worst of the bleeding. The old map table was awash and the blood was spilling onto the floor. First of all he sewed up the severed artery in the General's thigh, and then he moved from one wound to the next, rejoining the slashed blood vessels in a rapidly losing battle for a few more minutes of life. The General's right side had become nothing but a crumbling dam, too badly damaged for any real repair.

By the dim light of gas lamps, the General's staff, the doctor and a priest gathered around their wounded leader. His battle was no longer either feud or riot, it was one for breath. He could feel his strength draining away, and he wondered how one side of him could be so loose as hardly to form any part of him. He felt very weak but, as yet, little pain. He had been wounded before, and knew that the wounds would hurt later. He wanted to speak to the shocked faces around him, but his tongue had outgrown his mouth and gone limp. He was being choked by a jellyfish in this throat. It was getting colder and the wind of the cold highlands was in his back, the icy wind of old campaigns leaking through his injured side. Where was his flesh? Where were his lungs? Where was his breath, and where his mother? Then words came:

'Fetch my mother. Perhaps she can warm me.'

A spasm of pain followed his words, and he was filled by a sense of urgency. The pain had come now: there would be no 'later'; every part of his body ached, even his fingers felt as though they would vomit. His body was curling back on itself, wave upon wave of pain was breaking over him; drenched by a sweat as bitterly cold as mountain frost, he was being dragged by the undertow to death. His wandering eyes rested on the bandaged shoulder of one of his officers. Outside he could hear the battering of guns. All his staff were leaning over him: they wanted him to speak. Through the blurred nightmare of his pain he realised that he was expected to say something: they were waiting. The wind had run through all his body now, and he felt sure that he would never be warm again. Only one spot in his back was burning, eaten away in the acid corrosion of his severed flesh and bone. He was not even burning for his country, nor yet for the civil war, nor even for his side: he was just one of the many wasted in a crossfire of petty grievances in a family feud.

He felt that despite his youth and rank, his uniform and medals, everything was gone now: his glory and honour would be forgotten, everything would be forgotten – except for that one day of confusion. He was overcome with grief at the thought of having wasted his life, of having made a fool of himself: the fear of ridicule was very strong inside him. Gathering up the last of his strength, he spoke loudly and clearly,

'Cease fire! This is not our battle.'

He was full of anger at the Briceño brothers, who had used him and his love for their sister to sidetrack him into murdering the Beltráns when all he had wanted was the blood of Don Rodrigo.

'Cease fire! That is an order... and dismiss!' Then he lay back, exhausted.

The room emptied as his officers filed out, and, following his orders, two men rode into La Caldera to fetch the General's mother, while others sounded a ceasefire.

Slowly, the rain of bullets became a mere drizzle, fading into the odd sniper, and then stopped altogether – but too late for General Polidoro to be able to hear. His last orders had wrenched and torn the few tissues that had held his wounded lung, which had burst and spilled in a blubbery mass. He hadn't even the strength to splutter when the blood rushed from his chest into his mouth, so it just trickled out of one corner, closing his nostrils, and warming his neck at the precise moment of his death, coming – like his mother – to comfort him. His aide-de-camp waited for the priest to finish giving the last rites before closing the dead man's eyes. Then between them they covered his body, leaving him alone in the stale stench of the map room, before going to see what was left of their barracks.

It was dark outside, and hard to distinguish the living from the dead among the heap of stained heads and uniforms before them. The Beltráns and the townsfolk were already gathering up their dead. The wounded were carried into nearby houses and tended by family and friends. The dead were wrapped in white sheets and then slung in woven hammocks on long poles; and they were carried, shoulder high, down the mountain track to the town proper. Flares were lit all along the road, and the procession of white slings and bearers swayed in unnatural silence through the night.

Inside the barracks, the troops were murmuring their disapproval of the truce. They were still sore from their recent campaign. Press-ganged as they all had been into the army, they never knew what they were fighting for, but they knew when they were winning. That night they had been called off just when they were getting ready for the kill. They had been deprived of the best bit of their prey. They could have taken their revenge for the hardships of their march into the highlands. They could have used their bayonets to stab and kill, and that might have cleared the gloom and chill from their bones. Now they had nothing to do but scrape up the wounded, under a barrage of taunts and jeers from the village children.

The whole barracks was full of discontent. The troops were sick of being away from home, and fed up with the cold; they would feel better if only it could all be the fault of one person. Group by group, they turned on their dead general, vilifying his name and cursing his memory, unafraid of reprisals for this sudden mutiny: they had rightly guessed that none of his officers were prepared to insist on their loyalty. The same troops who had cheered General Polidoro in the morning, precisely for allowing them a chance to give vent to their violence, had now turned all their rancour onto his still limp corpse. The town surgeon had been right: there was treachery in the air.

V

General Polidoro's mother was at dinner when the two messengers arrived with the news of her son. From the moment that she heard of his wound, her own life began to drain out of her. She set off for the barracks forthwith, taking none of the usual things that she would have taken on a journey, however small. She made her escort dizzy from her frenzy of questions. When she set out to see her son, she left all her vanity behind, and all thought for her own appearance: Polidoro was badly wounded: that was all that mattered. She rode precariously along the winding track. Her horse was not used to such conditions: the road was getting more slippery every second, as rivulets of muddy water raced down through the heavy rain. Polidoro's mother spurred on her horse, and they struggled up the craggy cliffside, bedraggled and anxious to arrive.

As Polidoro's mother hurried to reach him, she came upon the funeral procession of the Beltráns and their men. Time and again she pleaded,

'How is my son? Give me news of him!'

But the town was in mourning, and they had no time either for the man who had caused their grief, or for his mother. She watched the winding trail of mourners, realising for the first time the extent of the battle that had claimed her only child. Sling upon heavy sling was carried past her; and each time, she was frightened that she would see her own son carried down. Each sling that passed her was one more chance for his survival. Forty-two slings were carried by, not one of them by soldiers. When she finally reached the barracks, the worst of her fears were gone; her son must be alive, or he, too, would have been taken to the town. She had strained her eyes by the light of each flare, and was sure that he hadn't been there.

She dismounted at the main gate, asking a guard, 'Where is General Polidoro?' The guard answered without even looking up, 'He's across the yard, in the map room.'

Then he spat out the thick paste of saliva and tobacco that he had in his mouth.

Polidoro's mother was glad to see that the lights were out in the map room. There was a single oil lamp hanging on the wall outside, which she took. She had made herself calm. On the road to Escuque she had panicked. Polidoro wouldn't want her to panic, so she made herself calm to see him. She opened the door quietly and tiptoed in. But instead of her sleeping son, she saw only the lumpy surface of the trestle table, and a room like the abattoir that she had seen once in Caracas. She raised the red, wet cloth, and stared down at his corpse; and lifting him to her, she tried to carry and cradle him at the same time. His weight and stiffness were more than she could manage, and he tumbled through her arms and fell to the floor.

It seemed that all that was left of her life was lost in the ensuing struggle to lift him to the table. Grappling with his rigid limbs,

nothing else seemed to matter any more. Polidoro was dead, and
she would bury him; he was all that she had. Only his aide-de-
camp came to assist her – nobody else cared. There was not one
single soldier who would help carry the General's body back to La
Caldera. She wrapped her son in the same stained cloth that had
covered him, knotting its corners over a strong pole. In lieu of any
other pallbearers, she would carry her son herself. He had never
liked to be alone. Not even when he was a grown man on leave
had he liked to be alone. At each step, she remembered something
else about him: days that they had spent together in their country
house, years ago; his stone fountain and his goldfish; his smile,
and his very first uniform when he had joined the army as a boy.
They had been unusually close; her wealth meant nothing to her:
Polidoro was all she had. Each step towards the town seemed to
say, 'Now you have nothing, nothing.' It was a long, long trudge
through the mud and the rain, half-carrying and half-dragging the
cumbersome sling.

She paid no heed to her bedraggled hair that had come undone
and now stuck to her back and face in disordered strands; nor did
she care about the tortoiseshell combs that fell like unripe cones in
her wake; nor did she notice the tears that ran ceaselessly down her
face, nor the mud that weighed down her skirts and petticoats – they
had come from Paris, and had cost her as much as her carriage –
nothing mattered any more: Polidoro was dead. Her wailing rolled
and echoed through the hills. Of all the stricken voices, hers was
the loudest. There were over forty dead, and the whole night was
weeping, but Polidoro's mother's sobs seemed to squeeze tears from
the very rocks and crags that tripped and tore her as she passed.

'My son, my son!' She had no other words.

The rain was heavier and the wind incessant. After the first half-
mile, the dead General's aide insisted on stopping by a wayside hut
to shelter from the storm. Leaving the distraught woman with the
corpse, he returned to the barracks village for a horse and cart. No

sooner had he gone, than the General's mother set off again, trailing her son's body down the bumpy road. Time and again, she tripped and fell, staggering under the weight, with no light to guide her through the night and no hand to help her up as she struggled with her burden. Before her, and behind, her voice carried and turned,

'My son, my son!'

She didn't even notice when the heavy rains caused a landslide which blocked the road, separating her from her only ally, the aide-de-camp. So she waded on, soaked and bruised, clutching at her soiled bundle like one of the many madwomen of the roads. It took her almost until morning to drag the General's body into town. Only the children were asleep that night; all the others were at the different wakes, and many saw her arrive like a wild animal escaped from its cage, trailing her sodden load. The General's head had been battered against the stony ground and his limbs were no longer stiff, but broken from the many falls. Perhaps more than on anything else, people commented on her dress: the mud and wet had risen almost to the waist of her skirts, and she could hardly walk for the weight of them. Her own maid came and took her in, shuttering the windows against the outside world. All through the day her shrill voice could be heard, breaking the ritualised hush of the town's own grief:

'My son, my son!'

Other mothers mourned their sons as well: eleven children had been murdered, and seventeen Beltrán men, and fourteen of their followers. The town was filled with the wounded, and the graveyard swelled with the wave of new graves. The troops were marched away, down backroads, before the funerals even began. The General's aide saw to the burial, leaving his leader to lie, stripped of his glory now, under a plain stone and a mound of earth in an out-of-the-way corner of the cemetery. The General's mother followed her son some five days later. Some said that she died of pneumonia, and some of grief. The townspeople respected her grief, and followed her coffin to its burying place beside her son, giving her some of the honours that they had denied him.

Of the seven Beltrán brothers, heirs of the first Beltráns, five had been killed at the barracks on the day that came to be known as 'the Massacre'. One more, Arturo Lino, was in a madhouse. Rodrigo himself, whose jaw had been shot away, recovered enough to be taken to New York for further treatment.

The day of the Massacre, in 1903, marked more than the many deaths: it was the first step of a slow decline. The Beltrán family and the valley were going down, hand in hand. They had first risen, long ago, like a sun over the valley's darkness; now it was sinking on the other side of the hills. Both the dynasty and the people were dying out.

VI

Lydia knew the place in Escuque where so many Beltráns had died, and she knew the cemetery in La Caldera where their graves made avenues between the orange trees. And once she had asked to see the grave of General Polidoro Africano, and the keeper had shown her an uneven mound with a simple headstone, very different from the granite and marble slabs, with their iron railings and their urns, of other graves. Later she had asked Diego,

'Why is he still so forgotten?'

But he had merely shrugged and said,

'One day they'll bulldoze over him to build a bowling alley or to widen the road. Meanwhile, at least he's left to lie there. I suppose that's something, nowadays.'

Lydia looked through the graves and plots for the name of María Candelaria Briceño, but she found no reference to her in the cemetery. Later, in the town archives, she found that only María Candelaria's birth had been recorded.

Again, it was Diego, in one of his rare, talkative moods who had told her the rest of her story.

*   *   *

After the Massacre, María Candelaria had been sent away to a convent in Trujillo for her own protection, and to repent. But the only thing that she regretted was having lost herself the chance of such a fine husband. Nobody ever quite knew how, or by whom, but she returned two years later to her mother's house heavy with child. And shortly afterwards, she gave birth to a son. Where the waste and the grief and the prayers had failed, her own motherhood succeeded, and María Candelaria became a changed woman. No one in La Caldera ever forgave her, except for her own mother, Doña Ignacia. And she was never seen outside her house. However, servants and the few visitors who still called at the Briceños' home, and the parish priest, and even the doctor, all swore that she had softened into the most loving of parents.

For three years she lived with her mother, and but for the inner courtyard with its potted plants, neither she nor her bastard son saw the light of day. María Candelaria didn't seem to mind, but the child fretted to go outside, and he would scrape at the plaster and lime of the walls and tear up the palm leaves and eat them. Nothing else seemed to amuse him. It was just after his third birthday when he tore the mottled leaves from the stone urns on the gateposts of the garden. His mother watched him, as she had watched his every movement all his life, and she didn't realise as she saw him chew, that he was eating poisonous leaves. She had never listened to what Doña Ignacia said, never heeded any of her warnings. There had only ever been time in María Candelaria's life for herself and, later, for her child. She didn't care about anyone else. She didn't know until she saw her young son choke that there was any harm in his wayward playing.

The doctor couldn't help the boy. Not even Doña Ignacia, with her poultices and her potions, could help him. They said that he had eaten the deadly leaves of the defonbachia, and that his whole throat was swelling to a close. But María Candelaria didn't want to believe them. The same girl, who five years earlier had watched General Polidoro's mother come dragging into town, and had laughed at her disarray, and the state of her own dead fiancé, no longer had the stomach to witness death, and she turned away, while her own son died. That same night, before there could be any wake or funeral arrangements, María Candelaria took her child, and left her mother's house, and left the town, and nobody ever saw her there again.

They learned later that she had kept hold of the body for six days. Six days in the sun, and the maggots had turned her mind. Most people had said good riddance and thought that it served her right. But a few had taken pity on her, and looked out for word of her from time to time. Doña Ignacia heard that she had become a prostitute in Maracaibo, and she finally turned from her. María Candelaria's name was never mentioned in the house again. So Doña Ignacia was saved from learning how her daughter became a drug pedlar, and how she made so much money that she built a brothel in Mérida that extended across one whole side of a square.

When María Candelaria died, in 1934, she bequeathed her new-found wealth to her family, but they all stood firm in refusing to accept any part of the inheritance. So the money finally reverted to the State. And the row of houses, with their pillared porticos and their blocks of matching shutters, that had housed herself and her brothel, remained empty for years. No one was moved by the sight of the decaying villas. Doña Ignacia spoke for them all when she said,

'We didn't want her alive, and we don't want her dead.'

III

THE EAGLE

I

B ENITO had often been reluctant to talk about Arturo Lino, his first master, and he would get sullen and angry if anyone spoke slightingly of him. He himself had remained loyal to this strange recluse, and he had waited for him after his imprisonment, weeding his empty fields, and sweeping his empty house for three years before he finally went to live with Arturo Lino's brother, Don Rodrigo. One evening, when Lydia had asked him what the massive grey millstone was doing in her garden, he had relented and begun to tell her the weird tale.

It was beside the old millstone that he and Arturo Lino had lived together. It had been on Arturo Lino's own estate then at a place called Tempé, flanked by a half-circle of outhouses huddled unswept against the morning mist. Ropes and brittle reins hung from the rafters, weaving in and out of the wattle and beams and the rubble from the roof. A muddle of sacks and stores spilled over the floor, and the mice were so used to this sanctuary that they would gnaw their way through the streams of grain and then lie bloated, from meal to meal and from day to day, sleeping sleek and careless through the unnatural tedium.

The decaying crescent of buildings surrounded Arturo Lino Beltrán in what he too considered a sanctuary: a place where he could sit without posing. Known to his family as a madman, and to others as a wanton murderer, he was neither of these things as he sat in the mornings on his own carved chair on the porch, or else on the huge millstone in his garden. He would run his tongue around his mouth, tasting the staleness, while long, dew-laden grasses brushed against the once fine leather of his boots.

If he counted the acacia tree and the twisted cider, he could close the ring of his home, and, more than anything else, that ring was his space: the only place he was at one with in the world. Not that he really knew much of the world, but he knew all the hills around him, and the lands of the Beltráns. And he had, at some time or other, wended his way through the valleys and gullies, and he knew La Caldera and far beyond as well; he had even ridden to La Guaira, on the edge of the sea, and twice he had trekked to the capital. On his way he had seen rich plains and barren dunes turned time and time about, and deserts and dust heaps, and villages where no one trembled when he drew near the bar nor pointed him out as 'the murderer' – villages where no one knew his name. They were strange, confused thoughts that he carried around his saddle on those trips; they were like fresh milk that soured in the changing air.

But that morning, as on many other mornings, it was the stale, sticky taste in his mouth that filled his thoughts. He wondered how the clear alcohol that he drank could become such slime in no more than a few hours. And he wondered why he didn't spend more time on his homestead as he crouched well-groomed over his stone, like some sacrificial victim, at the mercy of his enemies, squatting there alone. But fear kept them away and him apart, and his own rage and confusion gnawed at him just as the mice ate into his grain.

Soon after he had ventured out, Benito Mendoza, his lone retainer, and only vestige of his once overstaffed house, came shuffling his woven slippers as he carried an offering of hot coffee, which Arturo Lino drank gratefully from the carved half-coconut that he always used as a cup. Arturo Lino had few possessions, more through neglect than through lack of wealth, but he cherished the few essential bits and pieces that he did have. Among these were his chair and cup, and a Wilkinson's shaving knife that his uncle Juan had given him on his eighteenth birthday, then also his whip and saddle, and a battered pistol and his dagger. All these things he would clean and polish and care for, especially fond in the knowledge that they were all things that his father would have liked and his mother would have had no time for. The rest of his belongings were scattered around the house and outhouses in various stages of decay.

He still remembered the day that his brother Rodrigo had come with a hamper of food for Christmas and the dagger. Rodrigo had come to visit him then, as people used to do, long ago, and the two of them had talked of farming and families for hour after hour. And late into the night, as Rodrigo mounted to leave, with the aura of gentleness that was very much a part of his strength, he had shyly given Arturo Lino the dagger and ridden away before he could even thank him. He had held the blade and, watching his brother take to the wind, he had wanted to call him back; he hadn't meant to misuse the gift.

On the ladder of violence onto which he was born each man could be master by mastering extremes, but Arturo Lino lacked control, and he was alone in his confusion. Perhaps he, too, would have liked to have filled his home with children and the bustle of a working farm. But his days had become too long for him to bear, and his loneliness ate into his soul, and the wildness that they all held in their hands warped inside him, and he wore it like a cloak that he took into the town of La Caldera.

Over the years he had become the black sheep, in that sheepless country of goats and buzzards. Other members of his family were wilder than he, but his own loneliness and sensitivity had slowly twisted from misery to murder. And his failure to be happy ploughed through the hills, while his own ploughs rusted in his fields. Most of all he wanted his father, El Generalísimo, back, and then a wife – a wife who would be a friend. To be alone, for him, was to be vulnerable: the vultures knew as they circled his stone, and he knew, and because he feared his weakness in that land of the strong, he forced himself to feel stronger than the rest, and he grew more ruthless than any other Beltrán. Later it was other people's fear that drove him on. When anyone feared him as he had once feared them, he struck at them where his pride would not let him strike at himself.

Once he had begun, Benito took special pride in the details that he gave to Lydia. It was as though the cork had come out of one of his bottles of spirits. Everything about Arturo Lino had to come out, from his hangovers to his lovers. These last were mostly peasant girls who came and stayed a few days, and were gone. They left before he summoned the courage to be loved. Intrigued by his fame and excited by his physique, they lifted their skirts to him, but not their arms. Like an animal on heat he tracked them down: rarely did he want them more than once.

The only woman to come regularly was Ada, the washerwoman, who, in her self-possession, never gave and never took. He could always take her to his bed, but he knew that he took no more than his bundle of ironed shirts and sheets, and she no more than the small coins that she earned. She often came, across the hill, laden with armfuls of washing almost bigger than herself. Sometimes one or two of her children would follow her, catching at her skirts or just playing in her wake. He knew that she was proud of her children because they were natural sons of one of his own brothers, and everyone knew it, and respected her for having been the mistress of such a man.

Ada lived alone now in almost virgin propriety and her attitude to everything was one of disapproval. She held her head and her poverty high, as though it were somehow her divine right to do so. She always seemed to be bestowing a favour on whomever she worked for, just by being there in person. She often came to Arturo Lino's for the washing and the latest gossip, which she gleaned from Benito in the dark smoky kitchen. Under her thin, pointed features she held the secrets of the whole neighbourhood, and she spread them, with the towels and the tablecloths, gathering them together at nightfall and airing them again in the morning. And she had a way of embroidering any gaps or holes.

That morning Arturo Lino watched her come, tall and bony, flat-chested and erect under her washing and her tales of woe. Her long, fine black hair was drawn back tightly into a neat bun at the nape of her yellowed neck, and her lightly freckled face was drawn into a prim, pursed mouth, as though to make it quite clear from the very start that she would have no nonsense. Arturo Lino wished that she could darn his life together, but the threads were too worn and broken, and she had no time for the complexities of this man who refused to be ironed and packed with the rest of them; so her bony hands laid out his clothes on the veranda table while his servant counted them and spoke to her in undertones.

She swept into the kitchen clicking her tongue at the disarray, and she drank a huge tin mug of coffee and agreed on the general waywardness of the world and the bad quality of rice and potatoes that year, and she paused, briefly, to say in her high and slightly shocked voice,

'Compadre Benito,' for such was their kinship, Ada being godmother to Benito's dead son, 'Compadre Benito, what, I ask you, does a man see in a mangy dog? A dog will eat your food and give you none – not like a pig or a hen. Where is the use of it? With the sick greasy stench of its flesh in your nose as you work. Cowering with sad eyes and hungry teeth; I shall have none of their winning ways! Why, even a guinea pig makes a good remedy when stewed up for a fevered child, and even a sick child can shell beans and stoke a fire. God made everything for a purpose: plants to cure, their colours to tell them apart, and those that had no powers were there to gladden the eye, like the hummingbird and the orchid. But the sight of a half-starved mongrel, with its rib cage swaying on diseased legs, is no joy whatsoever to see!'

She gave an especially withering look at Benito's favourite beige pup. And that, along with the cost of living and the shortage of grain, was that; as it always was whenever Ada felt strongly about anything. Whereupon she turned on her heel, clicking her tongue, and swept out again, leaving a trail of farewells and pious hopes.

Meanwhile, Arturo Lino had stayed out on his stone, imagining, for a moment, what they had talked about. It was easy to guess, there was nothing new happening around that valley; there were new babies and new deaths, new wives and new wakes. Someone had his first communion, someone else the measles; rice was dear, life was cheap; he had heard it all a hundred times before, and it bored him.

II

He used to have hopes of doing something different, like being an inventor, or a sea captain, but all that he had managed was to exaggerate the violence of the hills. He concentrated it into his hands, and carried it into town, venting his anger as randomly and as cruelly as the natural elements did, as they decimated the people and the trees and the streams. But that, too, he found tedious. As a child he had once recited a poem at his father's table that was much applauded, and from then on, for endless years, he had had to do the same poem, with the same monotonous rhyme, over and over again. People would always say, 'Here comes little Arturo; Arturito, do say your poem!' But it wasn't his poem, it was somebody else's, he had merely quite liked it, but the repetition had made him sick of it, until finally the words fell from his mouth like drops of lead. He had had to spend his whole childhood with his mouth full of pebbles that he must let fall at other people's whim. They would accept his morose silence if he clowned for them from time to time. And now, a few years' wildness had left him out in the cold on his own.

Sober, there was just the staleness and the uselessness, and the buzzards waiting. When he drank, he was more than one of his father's heirs, more than a bundle of nerves, and more than a bundle of washing. And yet, he wanted his strength for himself: it was like a magician's cloak that he wrapped around himself. Deep down, he didn't really mind any more when others challenged him; but he had minded before and was expected to mind again: here were the pebbles tumbling from his mouth, here was the old rhyme pounding through his brain.

Nothing happened on the hills, nothing moved him; it was not his world. The rest of his family hunted and farmed, edging through the land in varying degrees of eccentricity; and, with time, they moulded themselves to the shape of the hills, and the terraced slopes to themselves. However, for Arturo Lino it was different. Ever since he was a little child, one of eight in El Generalísimo's house, he had had the uneasy feeling that he was already dead. He found corpses intriguing while his brothers found them disturbing, in the way that the wooden and plaster saints were. Only Arturo Lino seemed to be fascinated by their waxy stillness and the way that every movement meant a broken bone. That was what movement was like to him too – a supreme effort and a broken limb. His face held a twisted stillness. Other faces stared at him with the same shudder of awe as when they looked into coffins.

Arturo Lino's own uneasiness seemed to block his veins. Flies picked him out and settled on him, and their dew-coloured wings seemed to say, 'We shall stay here and wait, we know dead meat when we see it, and we would rather be here than on the dead dog down the road, for your body will make better homes for our larvae.' Arturo Lino was terrified of having died without noticing it; and when people smiled or nodded or even turned away, he believed that they were referring to his state of physical decay, and he would strike at his own fears through them, dispelling his own doubts as he stabbed and shrugged. They were shadows in his nightmares, ghosts of his own fantasy, haunting his escape.

Sometimes it was just senseless rage that urged him to attack; God knows, he attacked himself often enough, upbraiding his whole being with his uselessness and the loneliness, and the pent-up feelings that had no outlet but by these bursts of violence. Sometimes it was revenge.

On one occasion, in particular, a neighbouring merchant cheated him in a deal. Benito told Lydia how he had watched his master setting off at dawn with guns and ammunition in his holster, and kerosene and food on his saddle, and he was intrigued to know what was going on. Arturo Lino was gone for two days and two nights. His absence was commented on because he missed seeing in the New Year with his brothers on the Hacienda La Bebella.

Meanwhile, Arturo Lino had ridden all the way to the house of his new enemies, which was on the outskirts of Lara. There he sat down to eat his supper, and to observe all the people going into the fat merchant's house to see the New Year in. When everyone was inside, Arturo Lino barricaded the two back doors, and spilt kerosene around the house. Setting alight a circle of fire, he retired to the cover of a ruined wall some twenty feet away. He had five loaded rifles and his pistols beside him. He waited until the family and guests began to rush out through the only open door, and then he picked them off, one by one, men, women and children alike. Many burnt inside, overcome by the fumes, rather than face the unknown sniper. Others came near to him, only to be shot down. He left no survivors, working on the principle that wounded men might return for revenge – as he had – while dead men never returned.

He took his time to repack, and he took his time to mount, and when he reached home, he slept until late the next morning in a drunken stupor. When he finally did wake up, his head was as fragile as gossamer, and he was stiff from drink; he knew that word would be ringing through all the valley, in every hut and house, that Arturo Lino had done it again. He could just hear their tongues clicking louder than the hens scrabbling in their yards. They were making dust clouds. He would yawn with the weariness of it all, with the tedium.

He lay in his high narrow bed, it was the year 1900, the turn of a century, and nothing was happening. He wished his fellow men would do something with their lives; why did he always have to do it for them? Surely this was not the only way to raise the curtain on that small town's stagnant heat and make it move? Wheels moved, birds and clouds moved, why should they all be trapped in the unbearable stupor, the congenital inertia, of that town with so much past and no future? Even the buildings smothered the streets with their fiery oranges and yellows that glared in the sun and hurt your eyes until night-time. Then the same sticky heat drifted to the far side of the town, into the red-light district, with its toothless smiles and opened hands that soothed the stiff, disjointed days and each man's lack of life and reason, in back rooms, on sweaty sheets. The wives and daughters stayed in their trellised houses and grew bitter and mean from lack of love, while the menfolk paid to be caressed, and queued up at the brothels.

Arturo Lino sometimes went to the brothels, too, but he had never killed anyone from the residential side of the town. As he was always very quick to tell Rodrigo, he had never touched anyone in the family. All his brawls were in the brothels and bars. Not that his outbursts were ever really brawls, but he liked to refer to them as such, when he referred to them at all. But it was too hot down there in the red-light district; and, unless he was really in need of release, it was too boring. He much preferred to spend an evening at his uncle Juan's house, but of late, his uncle had not invited him.

III

Ada divided her time between Don Juan's and Don Rodrigo's house, bustling like a worried hen. She always felt deeply distressed when she did not know any of the ins and outs of those two households. It particularly annoyed her to think that even Matilde, the cheeky little girl who worked for Don Juan, and who carried water from morning till dusk and ate her meals last and had never a ribbon to wear on Sundays, might know something that she didn't. Nothing in the world annoyed her more than to be left out where gossip was concerned.

Ada knew quite well that she was indispensable to the two great Beltrán households on the two adjoining estates, as well as to the innumerable families of retainers and workers who lived thereabouts. She was a party to all the major events in their lives, and she knew all the little things that they did – and a lot more besides, if she ever cared to tell about them. Everyone liked Ada to be around when anything of any importance was to happen, because her mere presence suggested such immediate efficiency that everything seemed to be all right if she were there. And despite people's definitions of 'all right' differing enormously, there was a certain sameness about them all, deep down, that meant that the finished product could always be relied on to be generally acceptable.

The Beltráns were an eccentric family, criss-crossed with feuds and duels, gamblers, dissenters and drunkards, all farming and milling and tyrannising the valleys and the towns. But at heart they were like sugarcane going into the mill, differing in shape and size in every way, but it was the same juice trickling out, weaker or stronger; and by the time it had been boiled down, it was just one sticky mass – and that was what life on the hills did, sooner or later, to everyone. There were a few exceptions, but exceptions defied and denied Ada's own particular rule, for which reason she shrugged them angrily away from herself and kicked the stones of the path savagely in lieu of any other more accessible culprit to vent her anger upon. Whenever she visited Don Juan's house, she scurried up the avenue between two high rows of cypresses, her thoughts leaping ahead of her, anticipating the smirk of the living-in servants if there should be any news that she had missed.

It was in March of 1900 when at a summons she made her way to the big house, positively fuming with pent-up resentment. If Don Juan thought that she would come full of smiles and curtsies, then he had another thing coming. She had a good mind not to help at all! She wasn't afraid of him or the rest of them, she knew too much now to have to bow down. She had worked like a slave for them when she was younger, and bit by bit she had sweetened the bitterness of that drudgery that was the life of any poor man in those parts.

Ada had a feud with Don Juan's foreman; it had been going on for years. He was a sly, lumpy man. Some people thought that he had been good-looking in his youth, but drink and disease had changed him. He had once chased after her and she had refused – truth to tell, because his last woman had been a slut and left him, and she had no wish to take the leftovers of suchlike. Ever since, he had borne Ada a grudge which he dared not bring out into the open, although he never lost the opportunity of bothering and niggling her in private. She felt sure that he must have learned of someone's visit and he might even be foolish enough to imagine that she minded about not having been the person to give him the news. 'By God, he'd pay for it if he dared to gloat!' Sure enough, there he was, leering at her from behind the stables.

His taunts were more than she could bear, and she strode up the steps to the porch in so blind a rage that she didn't see Don

Juan coming towards her, nor did she hear his greeting of 'Good morning, and what do you say to the latest carryings on of my brother Arturo Lino!'

'He should be flogged!' spluttered Ada, 'And taught to wash his filthy dog's body before coming near decent folk like me!'

Don Juan saw his foreman laughing behind the stables, and, guessing the cause of Ada's alarm, he too was amused to see how hard she was taking her drop in the hierarchy of gossip. There she was, ready to burst, for not having been the first to tell of the violence. She would be shocked when she heard how far Arturo Lino had gone this time. Don Juan began to laugh at her, and coughing, he choked and struggled; then suddenly he was trapped in one of the nightmare-like fits that plagued his nights. Everyone knew that he suffered from terrible nightmares.

It was his desperate stifled cries and his subsequent fainting that recalled Ada to her senses; and it was she who loosened his high collar and fanned his face as he lay stretched out upon the polished wooden floor. Within seconds, the whole house was in commotion.

Don Juan soon came round. Gradually the muscles in his face relaxed and loosened and the rigid expression gave way to his usual mixture of frown and smile. His staff returned to their work and thought no more about him, they all knew about his strange quirks, his seeing things; and his nightmares. He was so scared of the dark that he made his manservant sleep in his room; even when he had a woman in there – which was more often than not – he made the manservant stay there, and a boy had always to sleep outside his door. Every time he went to the lavatory someone had to go with him. He claimed that it was to pass him paper, or to hold the candle or the towel – but they knew better. Why, his screams at night sometimes kept half the neighbourhood awake. And he would never sleep up at the big house, but always slept in a smaller house further down the farm. And yet hardly any man could beat him in a fight or duel, and it was only strangers, and fools at that, who would ever dare to challenge him.

Ada forgot her wrath at this sudden turn of events, and she listened quietly to the news of Arturo Lino's latest vagary. It seemed that Arturo Lino had ridden into town the day before, keeping himself to himself, as was his wont. He had drunk steadily at a small bar for several hours, and after a while, finding the atmosphere to his liking, he had invited everyone to have a drink on him; but one man, who had been talking at the time of the offer, had come up to the bar a few moments later, and ordered his own drink: at which Arturo Lino, incensed, had remarked that the drinks were on him and that everyone must drink what he told them to.

The stranger had unwittingly agreed to what everyone else who was present could see was to be yet another example of Arturo Lino's unpredictable anger. A bottle of the strongest spirit had been called for, and Arturo Lino had ordered the stranger to drink it straight off. The latter had laughed outright, imagining some kind of practical joke. But then the onlookers' worried faces and Arturo Lino's strange insistence had made him uneasy, and he had half-mumbled, half-exclaimed, 'You must be mad! Who are you, anyway?' At which he was told, 'My name is Arturo Lino, and you are not the first to question my sanity, and you shall not be the last. But allow me to mention two points in my favour: I hold my liquor well, and you may always rely on me to be consistent in what I do.' His tone of voice had been unnaturally polite, and the stranger, somewhat reassured, had matched his sudden courtesy. Thus it was that while thanking him profusely, he had met his death, from a stab wound. Arturo Lino would be on his farm now, sleeping it off.

Ada shrugged her shoulders, as the others had done. There were, after all, so many deaths – what did one more matter? But she knew that one day someone or something would come and cut Arturo Lino down to size. He was not a child, and no one had a right to so much attention. Everyone else's trials were subject to the hardships of the hills. No man could decide his life and carry it through from start to finish without disease and destruction taking over at some time or another. Why should he alone defy their natural laws? With time he would pay for his defiance. He would pay for disturbing the flow of life, if not for the lives themselves. Well, if he thought that she was going to worry herself thinking about him, he could think again! She had other things to do: dinner to supervise and then her family to feed, not to mention a whole mountain of washing that awaited her return.

IV

Lydia had met Ada, as a very old lady with eyes of porcelain-pale blue from her cataracts. Ada had a beautiful garden with masses of dark hibiscus trees, and she had a sewing machine, and rows of photographs that her thin chickens kept knocking down. Sometimes, in the evenings, it was old Benito who would tyrannise with his storytelling. He never wanted to discuss the likes of Ada for long, he always wanted to get back to the main shafts of his stories, especially to Arturo Lino.

Splinters of daylight were creeping in through the slats of Arturo Lino's shuttered window, they jabbed at his aching head as he lay waiting for Benito to come. The sheets on his bed were soiled, and he was sadly aware of his own incontinence. Years ago, he had had such plans about what he was going to do, he was going to be very different. The difference had remained, but the plans had escaped him; it was only when he sat on his stone that he could vaguely sense them. Benito came with his coffee; he, too, looked tired and had obviously spent the night drinking as well. He didn't drink rum, though, like Arturo Lino, mostly because he couldn't afford it; and then, he didn't really like it – not that he minded the odd swig from his master's bottle when he came home drunk. No, when Benito drank, it was raw fermented cane juice, brewed out of sight of the prying militia, and he drank to get drunk, like everyone else who went with him. Even so, his high-necked cotton jacket and matching cotton trousers were clean and well-starched and darned: Ada's busy hands had seen to that – she had taken extra care as she passed her hot irons over the cloth of the liki-liki. Arturo Lino thought, begrudgingly, that she probably hadn't even charged Benito. For years now, no sign of friendship had come Arturo Lino's way from anyone, let alone the chance to love that he longed for. No one would ever care, and although he had cared, his caring had become as warped and as strange as his own eyesight when the DTs got really bad.

He drank his coffee and Benito took the cup, fingering its carved form as he turned at the door. He cleared his throat.

'The weevils and beetles have ruined the corn crop this time, sir,' he said, 'and a lot of what was left has been damaged by the rain. It will not fetch a good price in the market, and I was wondering if we should sell it more locally and thus, God willing, cover our losses.'

Don Arturo raised himself precariously onto one elbow and he watched how Benito stared down at the floor; they had known one another since Arturo was a child, but none the less Benito would never look him in the eye: wherever he went, whomever he met, Benito looked down or away.

'All is not well, Benito, but I still have no need to beg. Throw the corn to the pigs and be done!'

'But the pigs died of peste, sir.'

'Then let the mice feast on the new grain as well as the old.'

Benito left the room silently and with sullen eyes. He had hired a journeyman to help harvest the corn, and together they had picked over and spread out the yellowy-grey cobs to dry, and he had sat for hours on the flagged steps of the veranda, separating grain from husk until his bony fingers had ached and stiffened;

and now that the grain was dried and sacked and ready to sell, he must unsaddle his horse and wait again at his master's whim for the gradual arrival of their mutual ruin. He would get no money now from the sale, there would be no new hat, no free drinks, no journeys into town. He felt that God should not allow his share of the grain and his share of life to decay on that ramshackle farm; but he knew that God had forgotten about that part of the world. He hoped that perhaps He would remember again some time.

Arturo Lino got up and shaved, scrutinising his face in the mirror: he had tousled chestnut curls, and trout-belly eyes whose speckled flecks had a wild look in them, that many mistook for anger. He had the high forehead and square split chin of the Beltráns, but his skin's pale softness had been marred by the wind and rain: years of excessive drinking had given everything about him a stale, sallow tinge. He shaved off the reddish stubble of his beard, leaving his unruly moustache to grow as it would. Then he wiped his razor and grimaced at his image in the glass: there he was – tall and lost; and at almost forty he had boasted like a schoolboy. Why had he told the man in the bar that he held his liquor well, when really he was so often just a crumpled heap on the outskirts of town? 'Let no one know.' His father, El Generalísimo, had claimed that the town was governed not by men or drought, or even by disease, but by the whispered rule of 'What will the neighbours say?' '¿Qué dirán? ¿Qué dirán? ¿Qué dirán?' they squawked, hovering like birds of prey, waiting for the least false move, the slightest weakness.

Arturo Lino knew that someday something would change – it had to. He knew that because of the wastage of time and energy, and of his own and other people's lives, and because of the tedium that he felt, the best thing he could do was to await that change. He wanted movement, he wanted people to react. As in the course of disease, he was a carrier, and he felt in his own body a torment of movement which he could not express. He had tried at first to stir up the sweltering, seething broth of La Caldera by subtler means, but nothing had happened. Perched on his stone, he disconcerted them with his silence, outraged them with violence, and waited for the day when they would restrain him, for the inevitable clash. And sometimes he tried to speed up the process:

'And you, Don Arturo Lino Beltrán, son of a great and noble family, domiciled on your own lands, did murder the woman, Juana, of no fixed abode, on the fourteenth day of April of this year, while the poor woman carried her baby at her breast...

'Because of your family, this court has turned a blind eye to your previous misdemeanours, but you have gone too far... Thank God, at least, that your father, El Generalísimo, is no longer alive to see this shame...'

V

After the trial, Arturo Lino was sent to a lunatic asylum: a long, low, barrack-like building. Two guards escorted him through the huge iron gates; and they left him in one of the single rows of cells. Many of them were empty, some of them had two or three occupants, mostly languishing, even rotting. In the cell next to his, three men were playing cards and joking. He wondered how they all managed, he knew that he himself would manage well: he had merely changed his perch from stone to cell, he was still the same half-paralysed creature unable to fly, waiting for the vultures to pass a verdict: to find him dead enough to devour.

He was asked at his hearing if he had anything to say, but he was so bored with sitting there on the bench trying to block out the interminable drone of voices that he could not be bothered to reply. When asked to plead guilty or not guilty, he had said, 'I am an eagle', and those were the only words that he spoke in all the trial. Although he was silent, all along the road that wound its way through the valley to the town, there was a muttering that was half anger and half gloating; there was a shaking of heads, and a wagging of fingers, and a pretence at grief, for the sake of common decency. In the streets and the market, tongues clicked like the chattering of vultures saying:

'Isn't it terrible?' 'It fair curdles my blood to think about it.' 'And with her poor babe in her arms, too!' 'Whoever heard the like of it!' '… And him coming from such a high family!'

And his high family visited him from time to time, and it was thanks to them that he was mostly left to himself and better fed and better cared-for than the rest; because all the families paid there, but some paid more than others, and some paid bigger bribes. When they came to see him, it was to see if he was 'all right'. He was their kin and it was, therefore, their duty to visit him. He longed for a real friend, and to be free of his family, of this 'great and noble family' to whom he could never wholly belong and from whom he could never quite escape. His father's cousin, Cristóbal, who was a tramp, had passed by his homestead almost every day, and Don Arturo had often envied him his freedom. Cristóbal was older than he, but from the very beginning he had done what he pleased. He himself had meant to do something else, something very special and very different, but his ideas had drifted and dispersed; he had tried to make them return, waited for them, and whiled away the time drinking while he waited – but all that came was wastage.

For all he knew, Cristóbal would still be walking by his lands at Tempé, past the ramshackle derelict of his house and barns. The hillsides would probably be thigh-high with the pink-tasselled grass that was sweet to chew; and the acacias and the elders, the avocados and the oranges, would still be clinging to the loose-earthed hills, or standing tall and shadowy in the dark sandy glades along the gullies, their roots thick in bracken, and their branches scattered with birds. The swallows would have hardly anywhere to weave now through the holes in his roof, and Benito, who was younger than he, and had always stayed out of loyalty, would have gone, or be cursing on the cold stone steps. There would be no wasted grain now, and no mice. Only the morning mist would be the same, and the millstone all overgrown with weeds that had seen more hangovers than grain.

Years passed, and the Beltráns were locked in their battle with the Briceño family and its aftermath. Arturo Lino never knew the outcome of the feud, nor did he know of the long trek to the army barracks in the hills where more than half of his family were shot and killed. He never knew, because when the remnant finally did turn up to visit him, some eighteen months after the Massacre and the grief, there was no sign or trace of him. And in the register, at the gate, beside his name it said, 'Don Arturo Lino Beltrán, nobleman, who is no more'. A guard who was standing by explained that 'who is no more' meant murdered or left to starve.

Much of their land was now left unfarmed, and many of their family were dead; so there was no sense of loss or grief for a man with no self-control and so little dignity.

The vultures that circled over the valley of the Momboy were squawking, and their chatter seemed to say: 'It's just as well, it was a wicked thing to do,' but they were really just squabbling over the carcass of a dead dog on the path; and Arturo Lino was remembered only by the site where his house used to stand, and by Benito, who missed him, and by his many murders, which somehow multiplied even further in everybody's mind.

IV

THE YEAR OF THE LOCUST

I

I T always seemed to Lydia that La Comadre Matilde moved like a bird of ill omen. At the age of sixty-five she still spent her life as she always had, wandering as cook from house to house in the Beltrán family; she always seemed to be swallowed up by her own shapelessness and bewildered by everyone around her. Matilde moved from job to job with her flapping bundle of cloths and petticoats on her head, and she carried a seed of gloom that she rolled and kneaded into the corn bread and stirred into the soups that she made. People often told her that times had changed, and that they had no time for her prophecies and tales of woe. But she knew that time was something that divided into before, and after, the year of the locust; and all the time after was just a slow crumbling into death.

Unlike most of the other peasants from the valley of the Momboy, La Comadre Matilde was both fat and ugly. Her ugliness reached astonishing proportions – giving her a general air of grotesque unreality. She was like a succession of loose misshapen lumps, from the bulge of her goitre, to the fat of her thighs. Many women in the Andes had a goitre, due to the lack of iodine in their diet, but La Comadre Matilde's sagged heavily on her chest, hanging down in a massive deformity. She had a large, toothless mouth, and an unhealthy yellow-grey complexion, and her nose was so wide and flared that she looked like a huge sea cow lumbering through the hills.

Lydia could recognise her strange gait from miles away. Even her limp was peculiar to herself – an odd lunge from her bad foot, where she had fallen through the plank of a makeshift bridge, to her swollen hip and damaged kidney, where an irate cow had kicked her, years before. La Comadre Matilde was coming back from visiting her old aunt, and her advance was a continual swaying from wound to wound, from foot to foot, muttering something under her breath all the while. Lydia guessed that she was muttering about the year of the locust, for, although it was fifty years since the plague of locusts had come and gone, Matilde rarely spoke of anything else. She used to nag the maids endlessly about spillages and waste, and each morning, as she rolled out the dough for the corn bread, she used to remind the entire household that there had been a time when the plain mixture of ground maize and water that she pulled through her hands would have been an unheard-of luxury. She would let no one forget the famine of 1904.

She would have been like any other peasant woman in the valley were it not for her striking ugliness and her foreknowledge of their ruin. She was often to be seen, making her way laboriously along the Camino Real, on her way to work or to visit her blind and decrepit aunt who lived in the hills behind Don Juan's house. This aunt was like an altar to Matilde, who was constantly returning, despite her own lameness, in pilgrimage after pilgrimage, to lay offerings of her most cherished possessions there. Everywhere Matilde worked, she was given little presents to bribe her to stay. People became almost addicted to her whispered prayers and rantings, and to her sullen dictatorship of their kitchens. She was more than just a good cook – she seemed to be somehow a part of the family, and every time she left a house, her departure left a sense of loss and ill omen. Everybody called her 'comadre', thereby making her an honorary member of the family in the hopes that she could be persuaded to stay on or at least to return later. None the less, La Comadre Matilde would just pack up her things and leave, only ever returning to her blind aunt on the hills.

Her aunt lived in a two-roomed mud hut with a low wooden

door and a thatched roof ingrained with wood smoke. Matilde would lay down her gifts, showing them off, one by one – the little gilt-edged bible, a christening mug, a knife box, a tea saucer and a sampler. Her aunt looked at the things with her blind eyes that were pale blue all over, and then they were put aside with the mound of other objects that half-filled the room. Her niece didn't seem to mind that her gifts were not admired, she was content just to sit and rest in the cluttered squalor of her own making. Every time that she went there, her aunt would ask her,

'I have heard say that times are changing, is it true?' and Matilde would reassure her,

'Everything is as it was, Aunt; it won't change any more now.' Then her aunt would lean forward, and ask,

'And have they forgotten the year of the locust?'

'They are beginning to remember, Aunt, you know that I won't let them forget.'

Then, and only then, would the aged woman thank her niece for her presents. Matilde would rise and take her leave, and receive her customary blessing, and go flapping down the hill like an ungainly magpie, remembering that strange plague of locusts that had come and gone on the 1st of January in 1904. They had filled the sky as though with blood, and they swarmed like clouds that hid the sun, stripping every field and tree, every green plant, until all the crops were destroyed and the land was bare.

They left in a storm of thrashing wings, and wherever they went, they laid waste the landscape, leaving a wake of shapeless dunes. Nobody had ever seen the likes of these strange invaders. The insects swarmed by the million, and they battered the people's homes, ruined their crops, and were gone as suddenly as they had come. The locusts had devoured every green leaf in the valley except for the ripped and tattered banana palms that they had, for some reason, avoided. That year there were no crops, and, therefore, no harvest. Each family learned to live around the stunted, sunless fruit of the banana. Planted to give shade to the coffee, it was never intended there for its fruit. It was too cold and windy on the Andes for such a tropical crop, but as a cover-crop it served its purpose: giving out vast leaves to keep the short-lived midday sun from the delicate coffee plants. Despite the inadequate climate, there were always hundreds of hands of bananas bunched tightly one upon the other, dwarfed by the lack of heat. The year of the locust and these unripe fruits were inseparable in the minds of all those who lived through it. The grey trickle of indelible palm resin became a symbol of their struggle.

After the locusts had flown away and ceased to hover like a threatening cloud on the horizon, the people ventured out. Looking over the debris of their lands, they didn't know what had hit them, they just knew that it had hit them hard. There seemed to be no reason for the sudden plague, other than chastisement from the sky, and many of them felt that they were being punished for the treachery of the Massacre of the year before. Ironically, the year that began as a sign of justice, ended with a massive loss of faith. The twelve months of hunger had been just too long, just too hard, and there were many who were filled with numbness, and whose feelings froze and never thawed again. Perhaps what was worst of all was that there was no one to blame.

The dead and dying mass of the insects was left alone, and everyone spurned their spiky flesh, disdaining to eat the brown, dribbling meat, little knowing that later in the year they would have gladly tried them. Indeed, later in the year they came to eat any root or animal – anything at all that could be crushed with water, and the juice drunk to give sustenance to their shrunken bellies, and ease their broken lips.

La Comadre Matilde had gone out into the empty fields with the other children, and she had poked at the dead insects with sticks. The valley looked quite different with all of its greenery gone, and as she stared down towards the town, she was filled with a sense of gloom that crept into her bones and never left her. She burst the fat corpses with her stick for a while, and then she left the other children playing on their own, and she went into the cramped soot-greasy hut where she lived, and sitting by the hearth she felt a great weight of responsibility seeping into her body with the warmth of the fire: she alone seemed to know that the valley was doomed to extinction.

1904 was the worst famine in the history of the country, and it stuck in the memory of the people, just as the dry earth had stuck in their gullets. Nothing else could be as bad as the writhing hunger of that year. The panic of endemic death and the hurried burials would long be remembered. There were days when their hands were too weak to shovel the earth. That year, the peasants scratched the land with their bare fingernails, searching for something to eat. Not even the customary mass of flickering candles marked their departures. And yet, death was not confined to the poor, since in the households of the Beltráns the very old and the very young died too, and the rest were weakened as never before. Coming as it did, so soon after the Massacre of the previous year, many families were still in mourning or even nursing their wounded when the locusts came, and the famine caught them at their lowest ebb.

There was nothing to fight, since their phantom enemy had gone; and there was nothing to do except face the famine, and slowly re-sow the land. The locusts never returned: freak winds from Africa had blown the strange insects across the Atlantic and then away again. The first crops after the invasion failed, but after a year, the land reverted to its former fertility. Likewise, the people who lived in the valley lost the hunger that had levelled them all, and they reverted to their former wealth and poverty, but the memory of their hardships lived on like a dull pain in the back of everybody's skull.

La Comadre Matilde also felt that dull pain, but hers was like a tom-tom in her brain. Others had tried to forget the horror of the famine, but Matilde, on the contrary, worked hard to remember it. It had come as a warning that many people had ignored; she felt that it was her vocation and solemn duty to spread its meaning as widely as possible. This she did, in her half-literate way, as best she could, by moving from house to house, and hacienda to hacienda, speaking from the pulpit of every kitchen. After a few years she would move on and start anew.

Her blind aunt in the hills and she were the only people privy to her campaign – perhaps the one-legged Cristóbal knew and understood, but all the others seemed merely to listen and then forget, as she told them how first the strange winds had come, churning up the loose soil and bending the corn, and then the locusts, like plague to an island from which there was no escape, and for which there was no cure. There seemed to be no hope of survival, and little rest in death, as the famine claimed more victims than the cemeteries could hold. Rich and poor alike spilled over onto the stony fields nearby, and many were buried in shallow graves on existing plots, making second and even third tiers. Not even the vultures thrived, after the first few months, because scores of hungry boys scoured the hills for their nests and eggs, and their numbers dwindled.

La Comadre Matilde never forgot about the famine of 1904, and she hoped that maybe Lydia Sinclair would take heed of her warning. Whenever she kneaded her dough, or made a cake or pie, she would remind Doña Lydia of how important it was to economise on the ingredients. She used to say that 'a spoonful of flour saved today could save your life tomorrow'. Every expenditure, however minute, always seemed like extravagance to Matilde. She was obsessed by the idea that the land would give so much, and then no more. So, contrary to local custom, she would turn one day's leftovers into the next day's pie, and everything turned up in one form or another in the soup that she was always making.

Lydia, a child during the Second World War, was not averse to this rationing – not unlike her own mother's.

Matilde stayed longer at Lydia's house than anywhere else. They fought a combined campaign on wastage, to a background of Matilde's constant reminders of how she had been forced to drink slimy water on the first day of every week, the cooked green fruit the next, and then chew on the almost poisonous, stringy skins on the third day. 'The ruin of a house is through the back door of the kitchen,' she would say. 'For us, the fourth day was one of fasting, and the fifth day would be the soupy slime again', and so on. Of her ten brothers and sisters, only she and two others had survived. Those who had died had refused to eat the skins. Matilde never ceased to remember how every fibre that gagged in her throat had left its mark, more indelibly even than the grey stains on her clothes. Her slow gait and dull eyes remembered that year, and the pain in her kidney and in her foot remembered, but everywhere she went people were deaf to her premonitions, and nobody but Lydia seemed to care that in the delirium of the famine, she had foreseen the drought.

II

In Don Rodrigo Beltrán's house, the locusts came as though to underline the weight and full extent of his family's disaster. Don Rodrigo himself was still away in New York, having operation after operation to restore his face. When he returned, in late 1904, the worst of the famine was over. He had sailed home on the Union Castle Line, carrying with him a young magnolia tree, carefully packed in moist peat. The ship had stopped to refuel at Port of Spain, at the ramshackle jetty on that part of the island that was known, incongruously, as Brighton. The ship's pilot failed to see the importance of the unusual currents marked on his chart, and, drawing up alongside, the whole ship rammed into the fragile jetty, throwing all the dockers into the water. The voyage was delayed for days while officials completed the paperwork and assessed the damage. Don Rodrigo sat in his cabin or paced the upper deck, feeling his new face, with its platinum jaw and grafts, with the one hand, and clutching the magnolia tree that he brought as a symbolic thanksgiving for his recovery with the other. It took him four weeks to reach his lands from the port, and when he finally arrived, they were not the same lands that he had left a year before – nor were they the same people.

Firstly, he was horrified to learn how many of his family had died, both slain and of hunger. Secondly, he noticed how everything looked sick: his sons, his servants, his friends, even the trees and the straggling young corn. His children were listless and thin, and their eyes were dull. The famine had crawled under their skin, and it sat there, triumphantly. Later, when they were well-fed again, it would seem to disappear, but really, it would just sink in like a streak of suffering that they would always have to fight away. The famine left its scar on the household, so deeply that for years any laughter there was without pleasure. For the time being, though, it merely took the form of a dullness in the children's eyes, and a lack of interest in the toys that their father brought them from New York. Not even Alejandro was pleased with the model cane crusher that had been specially made for him. He said, 'Thank you', politely, and looked away: the taste of stale boiled fruits, and the sensation of slime that they produced in his throat, were too strong for him to feel any real excitement.

Alejandro and his brother, Elías, kicked around in the yard. Their aunt, Delia, carried the burden of the household, and it was she who had somehow managed to see them through the year of famine; but it was he, Alejandro, who must comfort his father for his strange metal jaw, and soothe and amuse his brother, Elías, to make up for the nightly loss of their mother, who was banished from her own home. Every afternoon, at exactly four o'clock, her mule was saddled and she was led away to a neighbouring village, and every morning, at six o'clock, she arrived to care for the house. Elías wept for her, even in his sleep; and he clung to her as she left, every afternoon, through all the years of her exile. Don Rodrigo took fourteen years to forgive her for not having warned him of the ambush in which he lost his own jaw and more than half of his family. They were fourteen years of silence and tears, of which the worst was the year of the locust.

Lydia asked Benito how he had managed during the famine, and he explained that he had stayed on Arturo Lino's neglected estate for three years after his master's trial and final departure. But in 1903, when he was offered a home on Don Rodrigo's estate, he moved down to the river's edge, and remained there until Don Rodrigo's death. Benito was in his thirties when the locusts arrived. For him, they came and went like a scar in his gut, and a lasting uneasiness. When food became plentiful again, the people were careful in a way that they hadn't been before, but Benito excelled himself, hoarding scraps and stores obsessively. His room was always full of mice and weevils and stale decomposed food. More people died in 1904 than he could remember – what he did remember clearly was the death of the dogs. Some of them died at the very beginning of the year, when it became clear that the hunger had come to stay. Others, among them Benito's own straggling pack, had shared their keeper's meagre diet and survived. And yet, where men could live on the banana slime that was all there was, the dogs became sick and twisted. They were the first to refuse to stand up, and the first to lie down in the near paralysis that this lack of food produced. They had lain for days, filling the air with their barely audible moans. It was the slowness of their death that horrified Benito. He had sat and watched their listless, pleading eyes move in their already inert bodies, that were no more than heaps of jutting bones with the skin stretched taut across them. Their eyes begged for release from the torture, but Benito loved them, and he wanted them to survive, so he watched them suffer, thick with flies; and one by one he watched them die. Everyone's dogs were dying: there were those who minded, and those who did not. As the year wore on, feelings were worn down and permanently dulled a little.

*   *   *

Sara and Rosa Beltrán were the only surviving children of another of Rodrigo's brothers, Pedro. They didn't live out in the country, so they had no contact with the pillaged land. They lived cloistered in a huge rambling town house, overlooking one of the plazas of La Caldera itself, which from the year of the locust became like a prison and a sanctuary rolled into one. Sara was the eldest, and it was mostly she who noticed how their pantry emptied and was not refilled, and how their meals grew scantier every day, and how the house staff were leaving, believing that they could eat better elsewhere, little knowing that the whole country was going hungry.

Their mother, who had always been a little cross and had nervous headaches and backaches and migraine, seemed in that one year to wither into an age far beyond her own, and she became hard and bitter. Pedro, their father, had been the centre of the household; it was he who had played with and talked and sung to the children; without him, the house was like a dictatorship, in which their hunger was only one of many scourges. The end of the year found them warped and cut off from the world. They stared out through the drawing-room window, across the dying splendour of the town square, shaking the wrought-iron window bars with spindly fingers. Sara, at least, never lost the strained, sunken look in her eyes.

La Comadre Matilde waded through the famine in a state of bewilderment. All the rules and walls of their society had crumbled under the weight of the calamity. There was no knowing where she stood, nor why. Inside the stale warmth of her mother's wattle and daub hut, she and her sisters had crouched around the hearthstones upon which a clay pot with their usual green bananas was boiling. Matilde had watched how they turned from white to yellow to pink as they cooked, and she had rubbed away the grey gum that stuck to her fingers from the peeling. Everyone and every scant, battered item in the hut was stained grey from the raw fruit. In the course of the year, not a cloth or dress or scrap was saved from the indelible stains that stayed like hallmarks of suffering.

La Comadre Matilde was different from the other people in the valley in that she felt no allegiance to anyone. At the age of ten she had seen a plague of locusts destroy her home and country, and she had seen how no one had been strong enough to reverse the damage. Time took its course, her sisters and the livestock and the neighbours died. Only the dwarfed banana palms had saved their valley from extinction. She, Matilde, was one of the survivors, thanks to that stunted fruit and nothing else: her survival made her as strong and as worthy as any man in the valley. When the famine passed, she was sent to work, and she worked for the rest of her life but all the while, her slow, bovine eyes seemed to say,

'We are the same in trouble – there were no lords during the famine.'

She watched the coffee and palms give way to sugarcane. The bananas had saved their lives; she feared their going. For her, the change could only bring evil. It seemed like the natural consequence of their disappearance that the chill misty climate that was typical of the Andes should gradually change to the new sweltering heat that came and stayed. In kitchen after kitchen, Matilde worked and ate and prayed: she prayed under her breath as she stirred the beans and while she rolled out the corn bread. Nobody knew what she said, but all the children were frightened of her, and they ran away and hid whenever her lumbering frame came near them.

Ada, the washerwoman, had been stronger and more confident than the other peasants on the Hacienda La Bebella. She had a better hut with a proper garden, a real oil lamp, and fine children who knew how to read and write their names. Juan Beltrán had doted on her, and she had been indispensable to many households in the valley. She had visited them like a balm for every bruise and sore. She was relied on to ease every minor mishap. But not even she could conjure up food from the empty larders. After all the livestock had grown scraggy and been slaughtered and eaten, and the bones stewed, the hooves jellied, and parts of the meat dried or potted, there was nothing else that Ada could do. She couldn't prevent the meat that had been saved from going off, nor could she stop the river from dwindling and starving the replacement crops that had been planted after the locusts. All she could do was to sit at home, nursing her own sons, who were fractious and ailing. Matilde remembered her as a child. As the year dragged on, Ada buried her children with the other children on the hill.

After the famine was over, she stayed at home more and more, shut away with her only daughter and the one son who was left to her, who was weak in the head, and dribbled when he talked. She continued to launder clothes, but she had been obliged to swallow her pride, and she beat the wet clothes against her washing stone on the edge of the river, thrashing them so savagely that the cloth wore out and went into holes in her hands.

A shroud of despair fell over every household, working its way inside to form a hard core that never quite went away. The end of the famine and the struggle to survive came too late: by the time it came, everyone was like a chrysalis of doom. No one who had ever seen it could forget the upturned soil of the cemetery, so full of graves that it looked like a ploughed field, nor the bright carpet of dead birds that appeared one day, nor the agonised staring of the dogs as they died, nor the knot of hunger. For a whole year the sound of the river had given way to the low moans and the whining of distress, children had clawed at the earth and scratched at the whitewash and mould on the walls to eat it. The year of the locust had stretched over all their lives. If the Massacre had been their death, then the locusts were the battening down of their coffin lids, and the future was just the slow death inside them – an inevitable trudge to the graveyard. The rest of their lives would be a ritualised funeral; Matilde and her blind aunt knew that, but it dawned on others more slowly.

V

THE FIVE WHEELS

I

PERHAPS Benito's favourite character was Lydia's dead father-in-law, Don Alejandro Beltrán, for whom he had worked for fifteen years, and he had never had such a kind friend. He had known Don Alejandro since he was a small boy, and one of his most vivid memories was of him playing in the courtyard of his house with his little toy mills. He would sit for hours on end, working the model machinery. When he grew up, Don Alejandro Beltrán dreamed of the day when he could find and erect the biggest cane crusher in the Andes. He had inherited his father's estates, factory, furnace and mill; and already the immense red-bricked chimney towered over all the other chimneys for hundreds of miles around. It was bigger than it could possibly need to be, and stood defiantly on its great square base, almost proud of the long crack that ran from the top rim to halfway down. Higher under the factory roof there was a vast waterwheel. The wheel was built to be an exact replica of a nineteenth-century English design. Like the chimney, set among tall, wind-twisted trees and bracken, it had the air of a moorland mill in Yorkshire. However, no wool or cotton reached this mill: this was a trapiche – a sugar factory supplied by incessant trails of laden donkeys; from six until six they were used in a dull repetition of tired steps.

After work, the donkeys were led across the bridge to the stables. They reared and bucked under the vaulted cedar roof hung with saddlery, in a frenzied whirlwind of expectation as the four male studs were released from their enclosure, skidding down the hill in their rush. There would be about twenty minutes of neck biting and neighing and mounting, and then the studs would be led staggering away. Don Alejandro, who always liked to watch, would then bathe and change, reappearing some half an hour later in an immaculate linen suit, his fair hair combed flat with its washing.

Don Alejandro believed in multiple siestas, of which the before-dinner one was certainly the most important. He would lie back in a cream-coloured embroidered hammock that hung from pillar to beam on the flagged corridor overlooking his rose garden. He had a tasselled cord around another pillar, and by holding this rope he could keep his hammock swaying without getting up, and without having to call someone to push him. He would cover his face with an opened book or paper, feigning sleep and thereby avoiding any interruption, and, to the gentle rocking of his body, he would visualise the huge new cane crusher that he would find and install. It would replace the fine, but not nearly so powerful, 'Squire' that sat there now, squat and strained, dwarfed by the wheel and chimney that cried out for something as vast as they.

The new crusher would have five *mazas* – cast-iron cogwheels whose teeth interlocked and drove the machinery. Nobody had a trapiche with five wheels. Nobody appreciated the nobility of the sugarcane, nor the uniqueness of the giant chimney and waterwheel. It was not just a factory, it was a work of art, a temple of fullness and emptiness, a hungry void. Besides which, he liked sugarcane, he liked to suck and chew it, and he liked to watch its fluffy flowers swaying like elevated cornfields in the wind, and the shady avenues that it made across his lands, and he liked the clear brown blocks of lump sugar that it became. Don Alejandro loved the relentless power efficiently used, and to see mechanical perfection – each part of the whole working in unison, not like his own body that was so often racked and stopped by the mutiny of his heart, held captive by a tightening metal band. In 1933, at the age of thirty-four, he had already had two serious heart attacks.

Don Alejandro was three times Governor of the State, and he

was so popular that local people said that it was his kindness that had worn down and used up his heart. However, it would take many more coronaries to break his strength. He was determined to live and enjoy his friends and family and Diego, his son. And then there were his work and his hobbies: the guitars that he made in his spare time, and the trees that he grafted, and all his orchids. And there was Isabel, his mistress, who was beautiful and to whom he went from time to time, but who wanted him all the time, and who ate her dark eyes away, smouldering in her villa with rage and frustration.

People said that Isabel would be his undoing. This was said, half behind his back, in a knowing, worried way that was meant to warn him, but he just brushed it away like hair from his forehead. The only things that warned him were the unwilling beating of his heart and the relentless chugging of the trapiche's wheels, not nights of pleasure. Isabel usually wanted to fight. He didn't like that side of her fieriness so he would leave her furiously raving, and ride happily away. Then in 1934 he bought a car – a great black Bentley.

Isabel liked the car, and so did his son, Diego. To Don Alejandro it was just a toy, until Diego was shot in the neck in a hunting accident, and nothing would staunch the blood, when it had got him to a surgeon and saved his life, and then it became almost an honorary member of the family. In years to come there would be a lot of cars. Lorries would replace the donkeys, and jeeps would replace the mules that fed the hungry machinery. Children would still enjoy a ride in their father's car, but cars would become so commonplace that they could never have the thrill Diego had in that first chariot. Diego came to love speed in itself, but his father merely loved the toy, its black brilliance and the curves of its leather and the pounding of its engine, and its synchronised movement.

II

Isabel and Alejandro were distant cousins: more or less everybody for a hundred miles around was Alejandro's cousin. Apart from her family tie, Isabel had very little else in common with the rest of the valley. She shared no interest in the comings and goings of her compatriots. She had neither a husband nor children to care for, and, unlike most other widows in the town, she was neither old nor mourning. She was twenty-five, beautiful, and had enough money to live on modestly, which meant that her servants were usually even more underpaid than most, and her house and furniture were not as well maintained as her wardrobe.

Her grandmother had lived on Beltrán lands and had worked as cook to their sugarmill workers. It took all of Benito's tact to explain to Lydia with proper decency the origins of Isabel's blood link with the Beltráns. It seemed that there were numerous branches of the one family, a few members of whom were remembered for great feats, others for lesser and more bizarre ones. Of the last were Chappie and Cheo, two of Alejandro's uncles, who sank years of their life into systematically seducing the entire female population for many miles along the edge of the Camino Real. It was said that they respected the wives and daughters of their own family, and only wooed the peasants, but this was not very widely believed. To avoid conflicts, Chappie took one side of the road and Cheo the other, each claiming a hinterland of a mile or so.

Exactly why the plan worked, and exactly to what and whose advantage was never quite established, since, although many attractive women and pretty girls passed through their hands, a lot of old and seemingly undesirable ones also had a turn. Broadly speaking, the children – and there were many – who were born to the north of the road and bore some resemblance to the Beltráns were said to be Chappie's, and those who were born to the south were said to be Cheo's. There was much speculation as to what happened to those who crossed the road.

Isabel's mother was one of this rather large generation of peasant-Beltrán stock. In her turn she became the mistress of yet another Beltrán, who persuaded his sister to bring up Isabel – fruit of this affair – from the age of six onwards. Thus, although she was illegitimate, she was well-born, and although she had no dowry, she was well educated. She was also shrewd enough to realise that if she played her cards right, her charms were sufficient to hold some wealthy visitor to the house, if not for ever, then at least long enough to get married and become independent.

Isabel had always resented the fact that although she shared the playroom and ate with the daughters of the house, she could never call her aunt 'aunt', but had to call her 'godmother'. Also, while the other girls could go visiting and to parties and, later, to balls, she was never invited because she was a natural child. She was left behind to brood and sulk. On such occasions she would run down to the mill and, hitching her skirts, clamber up the damp brickwork splashed by the millrace. There she would sit, hidden behind the waterwheel, watching the labourers toiling or resting, and she would watch the black, greasy wheels that turned the cane crusher itself. She was always fascinated by how they came together like lovers kissing and parting, like last words flung to a moving carriage, somehow clinging to the impossible.

Now Alejandro was the first wheel, and she was the second. The wheels were moved by a long cast-iron shaft connected to the giant waterwheel just as the River Momboy was the shaft that forced herself and all the others to gyrate. The two shafts operated with the same thoughtless tyranny, producing the same hunger. It was a hunger that burned and tormented, hunger that would eat the arm that fed the sugarcane onto its rollers: touching but never holding, grinding down softer fibres than herself.

Ever since she was a child Isabel had been in love with her cousin

Alejandro. María Yolanda loved his brother, Elías, and they might even have married; but for her, it was always Alejandro. He was the most handsome man that she had ever seen, and he was fun. She had flirted with him, and he found her attractive. She was not family enough to be his wife though, and yet she was too much a part of the family for him to seduce her casually, and not lovely enough – anyway, not at sixteen – for him to overrule this latter scruple. Whenever he came to visit, he remained teasingly cool, and he would be more interested in the maids, whom she hated on this account. Isabel was not one to accept things as they stood if she didn't like them, but she was good at biding her time. There were several visiting merchants interested in marrying her, of whom she chose the one who was least distasteful to her. His early death came as a relief that was only rarely tinged with regret, when her long silky body demanded some form of caress or brutality. Then she felt that any man might be better than none.

After a year – which was considered scandalously short, for a husband – she discarded her widow's weeds and quickly found herself a 'beau', as she liked to call the young men who paid court to her. He fondled her a little under the intentionally unseeing gaze of her mother whom she had allowed back to chaperone her. Isabel had warned her in the most unfilial terms that she could come only if she kept her mouth shut and her back turned.

Although her beau did not ease the fire that seemed to flicker in her groin, his presence did succeed in arousing the jealousy of Alejandro for his, by now, extremely beautiful cousin Isabel. He set out to seduce her, while she began to spin her web around him. He could have been a hummingbird or moth to her, he could have come and sucked and gone; but he had rejected her, and she was proud. Now, much as she loved him, he would be her fly, and she would tease and torment him and then entice him back. She discarded her beau like a piece of dry cane fibre. Her life was empty but for Alejandro, which left her a lot of time to plan and scheme her game, and a lot of time to brood.

Whenever Alejandro left her house, the hungry emptiness surged through her and stayed like a dull pain in her head and womb. Then she would call her mother and their maid and walk slowly up the steep path towards María Yolanda, who was her first cousin and best friend. They had been brought up together, and María Yolanda had always stood up for her like a sister, and loved her as such. Apart from their shared childhood, the two women had, at first sight, little in common. María Yolanda could be neither cruel nor calculating; but they both had a chip on their shoulder that tormented them: both were caught up in a machinery of circumstance that they could not stop. They had both been disappointed, and they both carried within them a voracious emptiness that dominated their lives.

III

María Yolanda, who was the third wheel, never knew that she was empty until a year after her marriage when she was still not with child. Her husband, José Ignacio Beltrán, was patient with her, but the family were not; it was her duty to produce an heir. It had not occurred to her that she should be any different from other women – she, too, was young and strong. The teasing that began as joking banter grew to assume proportions of constant torment. María Yolanda's surprise turned to disappointment and then to guilt and shame. Her friendly enthusiasm alternated between flushes of panic and desperation, and slow-motion depression. After seven years of marriage she was obsessed by her sterility and her whole character had warped around the inert shape of her womb. She thought that if only she could miscarry or still-bear, her existence would be more tolerable; she would then be a woman, if only an insufficient one. But as she was, no sign of fertility showed or existed, and there would be no heir to the estates. She felt that she had tricked her husband into marrying her.

She would follow up any suggestion, however weird or painful, and spent a long time every day doing and drinking and burying all the things that she believed could help make her with child. The long tiled range in her kitchen was always cluttered with pestles and jars and saucers full of soaking plants and roots, crushed leaves and stewing potions. Their bitter taste stuck with her, brought spasms and vomiting, sleep and bad dreams, but they brought no heir. Her servants would mix up the recipes in the condescending way that they might mix a mud pie for a child. And yet, unlike a child, she was seven years married with no children, and therefore she was given no respect. She was a burden to the household and should die, giving way to a real woman who would have sons.

During her bouts of depression, she used to sit in a corner of her back drawing room looking over her husband's lands, and the mill and chimney nestled in the valley. The chugging of the wheel was a part of her life, it seemed to turn and fall saying, 'Have a child, have a child, have a child.' She came to feel strapped to it, and even her knitting needles tapped in time to its rising. Before, she had sat looking out onto the street as was the custom, and then she could greet all the neighbours and passers-by, nod and smile, and exchange minute scraps of news. But now she shrank back like an outcast, hidden from their sneers and mocking questions. In her corner she would cry a lot. She had learnt to cry noiselessly and to let the overflowing tension inside her well up in a kind of silent hysteria, which left her exhausted and listless. She fingered her rosary for hours on end, telling the beads, beginning with many Ave Marías, and ending with prayers for a child or death. She longed, in the half-light of her room, for disease such as so many people caught, and for death to release her. She had even been to visit several times in houses where fever and typhoid were known to be. But Yolanda would live for a long time, and the shawl that she was knitting grew bigger and bigger, swathed around her in a falling sea of cotton rosettes. The clicking of her knitting needles sounded particularly savage and desolate through the silent afternoons, like a smothered insect scrabbling for its freedom.

From time to time she would look out on her garden or the street. She rarely visited her home to avoid the endless questions. However, when she did stare up, focusing her somewhat vacant eyes on stray dogs or cockerels in the yard, a wave of fury would nearly choke her. She would be angry, the way that buds and blossoms now made her angry: the whole world was multiplying, and she could not even die. Only Isabel could soothe her, talk of her own emptiness, picking her way across the spreading fungal growth of her greying knitting. Isabel, the one woman who did not want a child, Isabel who did not reproach her, Isabel who still needed her.

IV

Even Lydia's husband, Don Diego, would leave his book or his daydreams for a while, and call Benito up to his solitary suite of rooms, and listen to the old man's memories of his father and his uncle Elías. It didn't matter how many times he heard them, Diego was always moved by the details. And he would egg Benito on, pretending not to remember, and he would ask such questions as 'Tell me about Elías's breathing.'

Through the misty mornings and the hot summery days, Alejandro's dead brother, Elías, could be heard breathing. If Alejandro stopped and listened he could hear him in that mixture of the mill wheel and the river, the hummingbirds and the chatter of crickets and hens. Sometimes every gulp of air seemed to have passed through Elías's lungs and been wheezed out again with painful effort, turning as the cogwheels turned, interlocked and then so far apart, but always returning.

Elías, the elder, had been uncannily beautiful. At the age of eighteen he had gone to study painting in New York, and even there, in 1918, the euphoria of the armistice and the glittering months that followed, people stopped in the street to look at him and make sure that he was real. Elías had sent Alejandro lovely letters on paper made from silk, handwritten in black ink in large italics. Alejandro was just nineteen then, and Elías was twenty. His brother often told him of how he must go out and join him later, and of all the wonderful things that he could see, of the colours and fashions, shops and cafés and dances. And then the letters started to come sadly and always with some reference to his missing home.

The only letters to mention his health were the very last ones to arrive. They came after his death, after his family had sent for him to return, after his funeral in New York. Those last letters took a long time to arrive, and when they did they were filled with a sense of falling, of slipping irrevocably downwards. Alejandro still kept all these letters wrapped in a black ribbon, and for five years he had worn a black armband for Elías. The paper had yellowed now, and he did not often read them. They were like the letters of a soldier who must die on a distant front. Set in the middle of that strange whirlwind that was New York in the early 1920s, his letters described the exhausting rush of drinking and parties, his studies and friends. He had written, 'I feel tired, but I am not really tired, just dampened, with a heaviness in my chest, and cold in my spine.'

And then, just a few days later, he had said, 'I feel the cold in my bones and a leaden weight in one lung, and change greying my window like a drab curtain.' In that same letter he had written,

There seems to be no end to this winter. We were not made for winters, and each day seems longer than the last. I am too heavy to go out now, and every breath is drawn through full sandbags. From my window life seems squalid, with its grey snow and the same people. It is the details of life that seem squalid. I wish you were here with me this minute. I feel sad and excited. I want to see the hills again, and the river, and the feathery bamboo laden with bluebirds. I want to go home, Alejandro, and be with you. We should be together; but the machinery of this city crushes people, it has crushed all the grey people on the street, and now it has taken my lung. In these restless hours while I wait for it to release me, I miss you a lot. Please think of me, Alejandro, and may you never need your breath as I need mine.

Your loving brother,

ELÍAS

*   *   *

Elías died there of pneumonia, and Alejandro remembered him all his life: so much so that he was haunted by sounds that seemed to be his brother's difficult breathing; and in later years, when his own health failed him, he felt himself turn with Elías – one cogwheel turning on its brother, and then leaning on other sides, turning to the sound of the river and the waterwheel, the wheezing and the soft tunes of the twenties.

Alejandro was forty-six years old when he realised that he had had his last reprieve. He had forced his body to carry on despite five heart attacks and his aching lungs. He had harnessed himself to life and hauled his reluctant body through the bumpy terrain of the valley, scattering his charm and reassurance. But in the January of 1945, he lay in his hammock, listening to the steady patter of the newly arrived rains, watching his sodden lawn become water-logged and his grafted roses struggle to become water plants, and he knew that he was dying. In the rainy season everything must adapt or rot, and he was rotting.

For years, Don Alejandro had felt that he was a central shaft, a ray of sun, round which people revolved. Everyone needed and wanted him, for he had the soothing touch of his forefathers. He felt that he had received his power from Elías, but now, he realised, despite his still being the State Governor, his power was ebbing. The rain was draining him into the river and the river was rushing away. The corners of his eyes became haunted with the hunger and the emptiness, and he strained under his refusal to surrender. He knew, too, what Elías had meant, and what Isabel meant, and what his cousin María Yolanda's eyes meant, when they turned to fire.

In his study was a pile of boxes and crates. They had all been prised open, and they contained the numerous screws and bolts needed to assemble the new sugar crusher that was lodged on the fourth floor of the mill. It had taken thirty men with thick iron poles to lever the pieces across the machinery-room floor. The cogwheels were some six feet in diameter, the whole crusher could fill his drawing room. It would take a year to mount. He didn't have a year to live.

Diego's birthday was in April. He was just twenty-four. Alejandro and he spent most of their time together, and they needed each other to an extent that neither could understand. It was often commented that they were like a pair of lovers. Alejandro's room had a marble floor and four windows looking onto the gardens. His bed was very high and of dark mahogany inlaid with satinwood at either end. His bedcover was of crocheted lace. It reminded him of the enormous blanket that his cousin María Yolanda had made, venting her hunger in every stitch. He remembered how she had fallen down the wheel shaft and been mangled before she was drowned in the millrace. After her death, no one had known what to do with her knitting, so it had remained in a great pile in her drawing room.

By July, the dark rings around his eyes had become hollows, and every breath was a concentrated effort. Diego grew sickly and thinner in a kind of sympathetic decline. The two men would sit on the edge of Alejandro's bed, talking and joking day after day, while both their minds willed death away. The war in Europe had just ended, and they discussed their cousin Gabriel's death in France on active service; and speculated on the end of the war in Japan. Through the patterned bars across the windows the sounds of birdsong and the distant sighing of oncoming drought, the heavy shunting of the waterwheel across the river, and Elías's painful breathing, crept in and filled the room. By the end of the month the room was so full it was smothering. Alejandro lay propped on his pillows, too weak now to get up; and too weak even to sign the papers that came from Government House. He spent his last three weeks in bed. He was particularly anxious for news of the war in Japan, and both he and his son listened to the crackling Overseas Service of the BBC, which they could just pick up on clear evenings. He could hear the streams of people coming in across his courtyard of damaged orchids and roses. He imagined that he could hear them wiping their feet before stepping across the polished red tiles of the corridors that opened out through thick, carved pillars onto the flowers. And then he heard the hushed, confused mumble of their voices lowered in prayer and grief.

V

Diego sat by the bed, moving between the mill and the house, climbing up the steep slope with the sound of the wheel behind him. All along the long corridor his head buzzed with the sound of his father's unwilling lungs, and every breath made him wince, knowing how Alejandro suffered. The house was full of people waiting for news; friends and family were all there. Alejandro closed his eyes and held his son's hand tightly. Sometimes he would hold his hand for hours and hours, gripping it till the blood ceased to flow, and he could hear Elías saying, '... And may you never need your breath as I need mine.'

The wheel was coming full circle, crashing down on him, and coming again. Beads of icy sweat gathered on his upper lip, and any movement, however slight, shifted his body and the room in a sickening plunge. Over and over again he was racked by the nausea of the pain, clinging to the verge of consciousness, he felt that every part of his body hurt, every limb, every nail, every hair. The wheel had finally caught him now, it was taunting him, 'Breathe in, breathe out, breathe in, breathe out,' while the machinery shunted through his veins, mangling him between its giant rollers.

Someone tiptoed in to sponge him down, and Diego left. He drove into town like a madman, and explained to the telegraph operator what he wanted. He wanted telegrams to Houston, to the best heart surgeon there was, and a chartered plane to fly him to La Caldera, to his father. They had told him that there was no hope, but he would bring this other surgeon, let him charge what he would – if need be, he would sell the sugar mill to buy his father a few more days of life. Diego asked for the American specialist to come at any price. He had read about him in the press; if anyone could help his father now it would be him. But the doctors attending his father at the house said there was no time. They offered to give him morphine to ease his distress, but Don Alejandro wanted to feel his last moments of life, he didn't want to miss anything, not even pain. Isabel and his family were weeping in the drawing room; and representatives from Government House and friends from La

Caldera were in the hall; they came in by turns and stood in his room. The whole house was convulsed with suppressed weeping.

A priest was called to give him the last rites; but Don Alejandro, who was revered as a saint throughout the valley, had especially asked not to see a priest, so that when the time came, Diego barred the door, bodily, and turned the man away. Then he returned to the bedside, holding his father's restless hand, and stroking his bruised hair he whispered, 'There has been an unconditional surrender.' Alejandro tried to focus his eyes on the half-light, he wanted to see Diego for just one more time, and comment on the Allied victory, but he could hear only the rumble of unleashed machinery, the crunching of metal and grinding steel. It was not a small crusher, one that would hurt him and then leave him some of his sap, it was a huge one, with rollers that would squeeze every last drop of life's blood from him. The rollers took him in slowly like a stick of sugarcane and then swallowed and pressed until only a dry, sawdust-like fibre was left. He saw the cogwheels turning, interlocking their teeth as they turned the machine, and he cried out for the last time: 'Diego, the five wheels are crushing me,' and then he fell back and died.

Diego held his hand for several hours more, refusing to allow anyone in. When the death was finally discovered they unclenched Don Alejandro's stiff fingers, and stripped and washed him with his favourite soap. Then they scented his body with cologne made from the malaguetta tree that he had mixed himself and always used. It smelt like bay rum, only gentler. He was dressed in a cream-coloured linen suit. The furniture was cleared from his room, and he was laid in his coffin, surrounded by armfuls of white lilies that grew by the river, and wreaths of flowers sent up from the town. People began to file in from all over the State to pay their last respects; they came, well-dressed and ragged, young and old, with bared bowed heads and red eyes: they filled the house by the hundreds.

Diego would talk to no one, and nobody dared approach him as he sat by the head of the open coffin. He could not bear to be the first to leave, he would wait until his father was buried. After that he would go and be alone, and stop the waterwheel that someone had left untied and that was turning freely on its own, creaking and working the empty cane crusher, thumping through his head like a series of punches. All night the people flooded in, drinking their customary cups of chocolate and eating biscuits and sandwiches that the servants were busily making. Diego sat through the night, and the murmur of subdued voices crept through the numbed walls of his grief, and he thought, 'There should be silence.' Each new arrival came close to him and mumbled condolences, but he made no sign of recognition, no reply; he just sat as though cataleptic beside the coffin, and no feeling came to him but the emptiness of his loss, and his refusal to accept it.

At nine o'clock the coffin was screwed down, and at ten o'clock it was taken to the church in the town. After the Mass, it was walked the two miles to the cemetery in a slow procession that packed the streets. People were walking fifteen abreast, and the long winding trail of mourners stretched back for at least a mile along the road. There were over four thousand mourners, who had walked or ridden, driven or flown, from all over the country to accompany Governor Alejandro Beltrán to his grave. However, most of the crowd came from the hills and valleys where he had always lived. This was the funeral of a whole era. Diego led the procession, walking and carrying, by turn, the heavy front corner of his father's coffin on the downhill slope that was the road to the graveyard.

Despite the general grief, and the slow swaying tail of mourners in his wake, Diego could see, in odd houses along the roadside, young girls smiling, old women gossiping, and children playing with each other in the dry dirt of their doorsteps. He looked with wounded eyes at these saboteurs of his grief. They were the very few who didn't know the man, and their refusal to mourn, even as strangers – their lack of respect for his father's death – was something that he would not forgive. They became so many cysts inside him. The whole world must feel his grief, but they didn't, they wouldn't. The dogs would not cease to bark, nor the cockerels to crow, and the hens went on scrabbling, bystanders talking. The whole world should stop for a moment in silence for the loss. After the funeral, others would forget him, who had been the best loved of men, but Diego had stopped at that moment and would never forgive the refusal to mourn of the unaffected, and the short-lived grief of his friends.

Diego was, by general agreement, the last of the Beltráns, not the last by kinship, because there were several more, but the last for his nobility of manner and his extraordinary beauty. After his father's death, Diego took the band of steel that had oppressed Don Alejandro's heart like a vice of pain around him, and he embedded it inside himself as a hardness of his flesh. As a child at the Jesuit college of San José, Diego had worn a spiked belt that dug holes in his waist as a kind of penance. A few of the most ardent boys had worn these voluntary scourges too. But Diego had worn his day and night, even for football practice. Remembering back to those days of fanaticism, he realised that the sores it made in his skin were a mere game. Now, after his father's death, he would never unbuckle this new belt again.

When the last spadeful of earth had been replaced, and the flowers had been piled in pressed heaps on the grave and on the neighbouring graves because they were too many for that double space where Don Alejandro lay, Diego left on his own and took refuge on the fourth floor of the mill. It was damp and dark there, and the millwheel had stopped turning. The machinery was still now, and only the millrace was moving. He stood there, on the edge of the great hole where the waterwheel sank into the river: and he stayed there for three days and nights. Nobody dared go to him, nobody came close to his weeping. When he finally left the building, he untied the ropes that held the wheel, and he walked away with the clatter of the cane crusher rattling behind him. It was the fifth wheel turning, churning up his emptiness, stirring his loss, biting into his heritage of non-surrender.

Lydia listened to the tale, and then compared her husband as he was then, aged twenty-four walking away from his father's grave, and as he was, now, aged forty, lying paralysed in the room above her. He had tried to ease the lives of his friends and neighbours, he had fought to defend them, but all in all, the drought had proved stronger, the land was shrivelling up and the dust had returned to the earth. And yet, he would be remembered as an honourable man, not because of what he did, but because of what he was. The Beltráns had been innovators, inventors, military leaders and generous men; but most of all, they were strong men who threw themselves into the thick of adversity, opening a breach through which all the valley of the Momboy had been able to follow. They were leaders in a land of impossible odds.

VI

THE HOUSE OF CARDS

I

L YDIA had listened to Benito's stories, and slowly she began
to place all the people that he mentioned on a family tree.
Diego's grandfather, Rodrigo, stood out as the central character,
but there were other, lesser characters who also interested her.
For instance, she was greatly struck by the similarity of the two
Beltrán sisters, Sara and Rosa (whom she herself had seen sitting
in their dusty drawing room, playing cards behind bars), to the last
de Labastida twins, who had also sat imprisoned by their window
nearly two centuries before.

The Beltrán sisters' father, Pedro, who died in the Massacre of
1903, had been both farmer and lawyer. After his death, their mother
had brought them up in an aura of bitter silence. She seemed to
blame the two girls for having survived the tragedy. In their skeleton family, their presence was a constant reminder of her loss. She
cared only for the dead, and she built a shrine to them with her
collection of porcelain ornaments. Nobody knew why she took
her two grown girls to Italy, whether it was to get away from the
places that it hurt her to remember, or just to buy china, they never
knew. But she kept them there for over twenty years, upbraiding
their weakness and taunting their fears.

When she died, she left them her rambling town house in La
Caldera, her wealth, and her hoarded porcelain. And she left them
the emptiness that she herself had felt ever since the day when her
husband and half her family had been shot down. Rosa and Sara
had longed to be free from their mother's tyranny. But by the time
she finally died, they were middle-aged and set in their ways, and

so withdrawn that they felt quite unable to cope with the outside world. They sailed back from Italy and moved into the old house in La Caldera that had been unlived in since they were children. They had been so long away that they had become strangers in their hometown, and they had nothing but their china and themselves to fall back on. They cared for this china with monastic devotion. As the years passed by they even sacked all their servants so that no pieces should ever get cracked or broken. However, they were then reduced to quibbling endlessly as to which of them should do the household chores. So they gambled at cards to see who should dust the china, and from there, they came to gamble for their every move.

They came to depend on the cards, on the ordered society of their Bezique pack. They lived in the glamour of the thin card society and for the ritual of the deals and tricks. Knowing what to do with their hands seemed to keep back the town's decay. La Caldera was exceptionally dry, and a covering of fine dust was accumulating everywhere. It was as though every brick and tile was being worn away, and the filings of their erosion were floating in the air. More dust seemed to settle on the Beltrán sisters' china than anywhere else. More than half of their games were played to see who would have to dust all the lower shelves and tables full of figurines and boxes, plates and bowls. It was a laborious job to keep them clean and free from spiders' webs. All the brightly painted snuff boxes, and the brittle Japanese vases and their rows of ginger jars, were smothered in grime, and out of reach in high-up places, such as cupboard tops. The windows had wrought-iron bars and shutters, and they were kept tightly closed to keep out the dust. Only the drawing-room window was ever open, overlooking the town square, and framing their family's decay.

Directly across the square from their house was the chemist's shop, owned by their own father's illegitimate son. They could see this man, their half-brother, in his wheelchair, at all hours of the day: he was like a deformed giant, with a huge vacant face like a wax doll, and instead of a hand, there was a kind of steel fork on his right arm. He seemed to have inherited only his eccentricities and sheer size from his father. He would sit in his wheelchair all day, frying liver in a pan, and his chief concern seemed to be pronging the pieces of dripping meat with his metal hand in a constant relay from plate to pan. He had very large, dull eyes that followed his actions almost mechanically, and his face was quite expressionless. All the while, an undersized, cringing boy climbed up and down the shelves of medicines like a monkey, managing the infrequent business of the shop. The grotesque details of the chemist's physique were constantly present as a reminder of their decline. This misshapen half-brother was one of the only four existing male heirs. Whenever Sara chanced to catch sight of him, she would look away, and tell her rosary, rubbing the beads with vexation, and thumping the cards down hard on the table.

Nothing had worked out as Rosa and she had wanted it to. The two of them had spent a life of waiting. They had waited for all the things that their father had said would happen to come true. Sara was ten when her father was murdered – she could still remember him vividly. He had been very tall and broad-shouldered, and he used to wear a faded Norfolk jacket with leather patches on the elbows, and riding boots that were made especially high to protect him from snake bites on his hacienda. When he was in town, he wore the most starched of high collars, and when he hugged her to him, his watch chain used to rub against her face, but she never told him that it hurt her. He was always the first to change for dinner, and when he was ready he would lean over the upstairs gallery and call his children to him, and they would walk downstairs hand in hand. Sara was tall and thin and grey-eyed, very much as he had been.

Sara arranged a sequence in her hand, beginning with the ace, and then the king, and then she began to collect cards from the pile, and then forgot, thinking about the stories that their father,

Pedro Beltrán, would tell them. They were mostly about their grandfather, and uncles and ancestors, and he explained to them, over and over again, how they and their many cousins had to set an example to the town and all the little towns around. He had said that their life would be full of dinners and balls, weddings and christenings. There, he would pause, and tapping the gilt panelling on the walls, he would say,

'It's not all this, you know. It's not all trimmings: you shall have power, and with it you must do two things – firstly, you must use it, and secondly, you must use it well.'

Sara still waited for the day when her father's prophecy would come true. She brooded on all that he had taught her, refusing either to accept the present, or forget the past. If only she had married, she would have had a child and heir – not only to the family wealth and lands, but, more important, to all their history. Through her own fears about intermarriage, she had not married her first cousin, Gabriel Beltrán. She knew that it was the intermarriage of the de Labastida family that had first ruined that family. Ever since she was a child, she had been pursued by visions of deformed and half-witted creatures inheriting her lands. By night they haunted her, and by day the sight of the de Labastida sisters withering behind the bars of their crumbling mansion teased her thoughts. It was only in the years immediately before her own death that she realised that the two sisters were Rosa and she, even though she had long-since known that the half-wits were across the square, in the guise of two shopkeepers. Gabriel had finally given up his suit, and gone to live in France. She and her sister had left Europe in 1938 because of the unrest and the talk of war there. Gabriel had sent her a postcard from Grenoble; it was a photograph of himself wearing the uniform of a French officer. The only other letter with news of him took eight months to arrive: it was to notify her, as his next of kin, of his death in action. Her sister's voice urged her to pick up another card, which she did, counting all the while the last remaining members of their family. There were themselves, and Alejandro's boy, Diego; there was the limping Cristóbal, the deformed chemist and a puffy, dwarf-like creature who kept a sweetshop on the far corner of the square. This last claimed to be their cousin, and a natural son of Don Juan Beltrán, who had ninety natural sons and no legitimate heir. It seemed a cruel mockery that all his other sons, including the three brilliant engineers, should have died or disappeared and only this one bloated gnome was left.

The chemist's and the sweetshop stood like corner stones in the town of La Caldera that had been established nearly two hundred years before by the marriage of two great families. In the middle of the square, on a rearing bronze horse, there was a statue of her great-uncle, General Mario Beltrán. He was besieged on the one side by their own ramshackle house, and on the other, by the crippled giant with steel prongs for fingers, and the dwarf. More than half of his family by direct line of descent were by his side: what would he say if he could see them all now? Sara was glad that he was dead and would never see to what depths the family had sunk.

'Your shuffle, my cut.'

Only cousin Alejandro and his boy had never lost their nobility. Alejandro had often passed by with a bunch of flowers or some pastries for them; and he had even brought them a little leather vanity case fitted out with china pots and bottles. He was so kind, they almost let him in, but he seemed quite happy, over the years, to just raise his tweed cap, and later his boater, and, later still, his panama hat to them from the pavement. When he died, they had ventured out for the first time in six years, and walked behind his coffin at his funeral. During the funeral Mass, they were horrified to see that they knew so few people in all the great crowd. Their father had promised them that they would be like queens of the valley, yet it was clear that the only crowns and sceptres were painted on their playing cards, and their only chance to mix with royalty was while they played Bezique. They never played any other game but this one that had grown out of the French court: it was the game of the cavaliers, a game of waiting between battles.

From the day that Alejandro Beltrán died to the day they died, the two sisters wore heavy mourning. They wore it not only for their cousin, but for all the people that they missed, and for the way of life that had gone for ever; and Sara wore it for Gabriel, and for the death of the family that their own spinsterhood had helped to wipe out. They played their lives in threes and twos, under the tumult of the painted ceiling, surrounded by their dusty porcelain. They shuffled and dealt, dealt and played, with the alacrity of card sharps. Nothing short of a lost card could perturb or stop their game. Storms and heatwaves, tremors and fevers, shook past them, leaving as much trace as the delivery boy, or the plumber.

Rosa declared a double Bezique, and the game was over. It was two knaves of diamonds and two queens of spades: days could go by without such a combination coming up in any game. It was a good omen when it happened, like a repetition of the first marriage between the two wandering Beltrán brothers and the two de Labastida twins, like their own release from their crumbling prison of a house. They, too, sat by the window, day in, day out, two sisters waiting for fairytale princes to ride up and change their lives. It had happened once before in their family when it had become degenerate and almost extinct: and it happened within the rigid rules of their game. Why shouldn't it happen to them? Meanwhile, they just waited and whiled away the time. It was Sara's turn to sweep up. She gathered up all the specks and flakes of musty peeling plaster and a quantity of dust onto the metal sheet that was always used as a dustpan. It was her turn to shuffle and deal, and Rosa's to cut the pack. She dealt three cards and then two and then three – as they always did; and then she turned up the trump card, which was a club, and the tea-time game commenced.

II

The sweetshop man across the road had a club foot. He had only come to La Caldera while they were abroad. On their return, they had tried, absentmindedly, to make up for a lifetime of isolation by visiting their neighbours. However, the necessity of having their visits returned soon altered their plans. No one must come into their house – even being out for a few hours made them panicky about any possible breakages in their absence. They had been informed, on one of their visits, of their kinship to the owner of the sweetshop, and the two of them had gone to see him. Rosa seemed unperturbed, even bored by him, and she had turned on her heel and left; but Sara was both fascinated and horrified by what she saw, and she lingered inside his shop.

From the outside, the sweetshop was just another semi-derelict building sloping back from the square. Yet once inside, it managed to alter every normal sense of proportion. It was a huge, vaulted room like a warehouse that seemed to swallow up intruders. It was dark and completely empty except for a minute counter in the far corner. The shopkeeper himself, who was a dwarf, stood behind the counter; his face and hands were so puffy that the pale distended skin seemed to be labouring to keep in some strange disease about to burst through and spill out at any moment. Sara watched his reptilian movements, wondering how this grotesque man could possibly be a son of Juan Beltrán. Their family had always been so good-looking – how could it have degenerated into this?

The shopkeeper's eye defied her aggressively, guessing a part of her thoughts. His eyes were scarcely visible, they were so small, and they darted under the transparent bags that nearly covered them. His bluish skin seemed to throb continuously, giving him the appearance of a tray of fresh lights in a butcher's. Only his head and arms were visible above the counter, and his stubby, swollen fingers drummed the fly-ridden counter top, impatient for the

woman in front of him either to speak out or go away. Sara couldn't
bear to give her real reasons for visiting his shop, so she ordered
half a kilo of gingerbread, and made ready to leave. His bloated
hands wrapped the stale cake in a piece of soiled brown paper with
such alacrity that all the flies on it were shaken to the floor. Neither of the sisters ever went back to the sweetshop, but whenever
they looked out of their window, it was clearly visible. The Beltrán
family had always harboured and bred extremes: once, they had
all been proud of it. Now, the bloated sweetshop keeper, who was
like a long-drowned child, fermenting on the verge of explosion,
held down one corner of the square, while their crippled giant of
a half-brother held down the other. The two sisters were trapped
between the two, locked within their own failure. They were still
waiting for something to happen.

'A common marriage!'

They were saving their strength for just such an event as this.

'Bezique; pick up, Sara.'

Sara picked up an ace, played four aces. She picked up her eight
cards, and played the last eight tricks following suit or throwing
away each time. There was never any choice at the end of the game.
For once, she had managed to win a game, so Rosa had to go to the
kitchen and make the tea.

The rub of Rosa's wrists against the edge of the table threatened
to bring out the spitefulness that she felt under her skin. She hated
losing: she felt that she had missed out on so much in her life, she
just couldn't bear to have to lose at cards as well. Luckily for her,
Sara usually lost – it wasn't surprising really, considering that she
spent half her life daydreaming and staring out of the window. She
herself couldn't be bothered to watch the neighbouring houses, or
the people going by: the whole town was crumbling – it was bad
enough to have the dust over all their china, without having to
watch the actual erosion of every brick.

Tea was Rosa's favourite meal: it seemed almost worthwhile

losing the tea-time game just to have control of the cakes and sandwiches that they always ate. Sara hardly ever ate anything anyway,
so she often skimped on the sandwich fillings, and the sizes of the
slices. Rosa piled the cinnamon biscuits and poundcake onto the
cake stand, in pretty symmetrical patterns. She had carefully cut
everything into special shapes, and was divided between eating
the corners and off-cuts, and arranging them as neatly as she could.
She wiped the cups until they shone, and then served the tea with
lemon. She wheeled the trolley down the dank musty corridor to
the drawing room, carefully avoiding all the clutter. She thought,
delightedly, that no outsider could possibly get down their corridor
without knocking over at least the low table of shepherdesses that
jutted out halfway along. She guessed, rightly, that her sister would
be staring out towards the chemist's shop when she came in. As
usual, Sara hardly touched her tea.

Rosa's impatient 'You to cut' began a new game. Sara spent most
of her time staring out of the window, like a prisoner surveying
the prison yard. She had spent her childhood pressed up against
the cracks in the window shutter, looking out with longing at the
forbidden world outside. Sara would neither eat nor sleep: she was
wasted and alone, watchful and timid at once.

The two sisters' house was like an hourglass, and the passing
of time could be measured in the level of dust and sand that accu-
mulated on every surface. Playing cards turned on the table until
their painted faces faded and wore thin; then another pack would
come into use and reign as favourite until it, too, was fingered to
death. Each day followed the last in identical fashion. Sara felt as
though she were holding a corner of a huge tent – the other two
corners were held by the chemist and her cousin, the shopkeeper,
while the fourth corner flapped in the wind. Her other cousin,
Cristóbal, limped by from time to time to make sure that none of
them let go. Sara knew that her strength was failing, and that her
only hope lay in staying exactly as she was – one move and the

precious cloth would be lost, and the cloth of the tent was all that was left to shield them from the desert wind and the sun. So, while Rosa ate until she could eat no more, Sara upheld the monotony of her own exile, and strove to ensure that the sameness remained unchanged.

There was a sameness in everything; and, everywhere in the house and square, Sara's staring eyes measured its presence. The arrival of the delivery boy was the same, although the boy himself changed many times over the years. It was the same scrawny brown hand that stretched their packages through the half-closed door; and in the dim light of the hall, it was the same collection of boxes with their spilt rice and lentils; and the groceries were always the same second-best for these sisters who always paid their bills, but never chose their wares. The same weeds grew around the statue of General Mario Beltrán in the square, and their desert blooms never varied. The chemist, with his empty gaze and his pieces of fried liver, never changed; and the little boy who worked for him and had his head shaved, and climbed like a frightened monkey up and down the cluttered shelves, never grew, but just became old and wizened, scuttling about his master's business.

Sara had watched them carefully, and yet had never managed to find out what kept the stunted servant there, nor yet what it was that he so feared in his master's behaviour. The chemist never seemed either to move or speak; even so, his silent tyranny remained unchanged. Everything stayed the same: even alterations came with such imperceptible shifts that their very presence slipped into the sameness of before. The climate seemed to have grown hotter, the landscape more bare, and the people fewer; but the parcels of sweetmeats from the sweetshop across the square remained the same. Rosa unwrapped the sticky paper, and picked off the flies, and ate the sugary mess just the same, and her waistline grew fatter and disappeared until all her body seemed the same. And the heads of their statuettes sticking out from under the dust were the same; and

Sara's longing for someone to love was the same; and the Bezique cards on the table were the same; and so it remained through the twenty-year tedium of their life in the town of La Caldera.

III

Rosa stared across the card table at her ageing sister. It was six o'clock, tea was finished, and Rosa had over-eaten, as she always did. Where Rosa had grown fat, her sister had grown thin. The cards and markers were ready on the table again. Spades were trumps and the game commenced. Rosa tried and failed to attract her sister's attention. She felt irredeemably left out of her sister's thoughts and of life in general; yet she didn't seem to mind. Her own thoughts rallied feebly and then dispersed: it was strange how little and how much they understood each other.

'It's me to play,' she said, rearranging her newly dealt hand.

It was usually her to play. Rosa held four kings in her hand, while her sister held four knaves – they both wanted to declare them.

Rosa didn't seem herself that day, she seemed to be even more bothered than usual by the heat, and no amount of fanning could relieve her. Stifling under the eiderdown of her own flesh, she gasped for air, struggling with the wave of panic and pain that gripped her chest; then she slumped back in a deep sleep. Sara watched her, wondering why she suffered such fits of indigestion. Two hours had gone by, and Sara's eyes were aching from looking out over the square; nothing had changed, but she felt inside her a stirring as though something would – and deep down, she hoped that it would be for the better. It was just before sunset when Cristóbal trudged by with his staff and his prophet's head of hair. He usually came limping by at about this time, but, despite their kinship, he always ignored Rosa and herself; so, it was to her great amazement that that evening he actually stopped in front of their window, and he nodded to them before slowly moving on. Sara felt her body glow with pleasure: something was about to happen without her having let go – here was the special day that she had waited for. Rosa and she had never shared anything but protection in numbers: they were both less vulnerable when they shielded each other; yet Sara thought then that, despite their differences, her sister was all she had, and, in her own way, she loved her – when she awoke, she would tell her so – so she rose to waken her, and share the coming change.

Sara shook her sister by the shoulder, and as her hand jerked stiffly to and fro, she realised that the change had come indeed: Rosa was dead. She released the mass of dead flesh that she held in her hand, and straightened her sister's dress, and closed her eyes, then she sat down and stared out at the square. She decided to call in the first person to pass by their house in the street that night; the hours struck on the cathedral clock, but nobody came. The chemist's shop was closed, and the sweetshop was in darkness. She toyed with the idea of going across and asking for assistance, but the thought of the stench of stale liver and rancid fat, and the idea of the chemist's steel claw consoling her, dissuaded her. By midnight, no passer-by had come, and Rosa's dead body filled the rocking chair. Sara tried to shake the inert flesh back to life, but felt nothing but dead weight and their mother's outraged voice scolding, 'Sara, you are forgetting your station.'

You had to follow suit in the last seven tricks before the end, it said so on the backs of their markers. Now Rosa was dead Sara would have to follow suit.

Having decided what to do she still had to decide how to do it. Rosa had died easily, and her sister wished for a similar death, but she foresaw that her last hours would be as slow and tortuous as her life had been. She had never been one for sudden movements, and there would be none now: no shot or stab would hasten her last breath, everything must remain the same. The night trailed by, and yet Sara could not decide on the time or means of her last trick. Just as she had done all through her life, she was holding out for one last chance, hoping for some reprieve. Wandering aimlessly through the thick dust and the clutter of her house, she chose poison, and she found and carried down the old household cabinet where the poisons were kept.

Inside the cabinet, there was a jumbled collection of bottles and jars, mostly empty save for a whiff of stale powder or a trace of dark gum stuck to the bottom. The laudanum and the arsenic, the chloroform and the morphine were all empty, the silver nitrate and the copper sulphate had long since spilt, leaving only a chipped bottle of discoloured sulphur that was burned to keep away bats, and white antimony that had been used to rub down horses. She knew that somewhere there was a jar of bitter almonds that Rosa had gathered from the misshapen tree in their garden, but she couldn't remember where she had put it. The old tree had never given any fruits before, but last year it had flowered on one side, and Rosa had gathered the nuts that set.

Sara thought bitterly that Rosa had always managed to win the last trick and set the terms for the final countdown. And it had always been her own fate to follow suit or throw away. She wanted Rosa to wake up and show her where the almonds were. Sara rummaged through the poisons, sickened by this final proof of her losing streak. She would have to abandon the bitter almonds to follow Rosa's lead. She mixed herself a potion of cold tea and antimony, and then she fingered the Minton cup, wishing that instead the bronze horse from the square would ride in and be rubbed down with this potion of tartar emetic that she had prepared for herself, but was so reluctant to swallow.

She lit a lamp and, turning the flame up to its maximum, watched how a green shadow invaded her dead sister's nose from the inside. Gently, she took the four kings from Rosa's hand, and, sandwiched in between the heat and her cup of poison, she played her last game of Bezique. Her right hand played against her left, and her right hand won; so she took the winning hand to her lips and swallowed the long draught of antimony and lay back to watch the morning coming through the window bars.

IV

Across the table from her, her grey-green sister seemed to be sleeping, but Sara knew that her fat gut was fermenting. A gnawing pain scratched inside her, and she reached out and held Rosa's stiff hand in her own bony fingers. From the moment of her first bout of pain until the moment of her death, every sensation that managed to penetrate her consciousness came on successive waves of well-aimed punches. There were rats and hot gravel inside her, and cold lead in her veins for blood. She thought she heard Rosa snoring through the early stages of decomposition, and she heard the sizzling of the chemist's liver and the neighing of the General's horse and the groom's warning: 'Don't ever touch the antimony!' All the china in her house seemed to be falling to the floor, in threes and twos, and the painted cherubim on the ceiling were winking at her, obscenely, and a whirlpool of nausea tore at her insides. Only the long years of training in self-control kept her from screaming, and her overriding desire for sameness stopped her from being sick.

It was only when the sun changed sides, and the dead hours were approaching, that Sara managed to leave her pain behind her, and really begin to slip. Both her life and her suicide had been a slow death, but, in the dead heat of the afternoon, she felt the corner of the cloth tent that she had held for so many years drag away; as it swept into the sky, it flapped like a banner, fanning fresh gusts of air into Sara's stagnant house, and the breeze began to move the piles of sand. Gabriel and her mother and father were all under the sand, half-buried with everyone else she had ever known; she herself had lived on top of them, she had grown old and empty over them, straining at every wrinkle, and stretched over more hopes and anguish than she could bear. She had saved herself in self-contained silence, and she had stored up everything that came near her. Now, at the hour of her death, she needed to burst and scatter, like a withered puffball, she needed to explode to justify her life. Instead, she just slumped forwards, and a small clot from her gut spilled down her long black dress and chair leg in a final posthumous evacuation. That was the only bursting that her body did – for the rest, she just rotted over the tabletop together with her sister.

Nobody knew how many days it was before the two bodies were discovered: some said days, and some said a week. However long it was, it took longer still for the stench of their dead flesh to leave the town, and the increase of flies and vultures seemed to stay, and no amount of creosote would induce them to decamp.

The two women were buried, and their whole rambling house was sealed. No will was read and no heirs came to lay claim to the dust and woodworm, the spiders and the china; so first the rats, and then the local children, broke in and roamed around the cluttered shambles of their house. First little and then larger trophies were pilfered, and finally, the doors were broken down, and the two sisters' porcelain was scattered across the length and breadth of La Caldera, from the Calle Vargas to the Camino Real. Children played with their eighteenth-century dolls, and when their porcelain heads broke, they would go back for more; likewise, the trinkets and flowers and all the statuettes were smashed and discarded. Mangy dogs ate from the glazed jelly dishes, and hens pecked at their stale grain from troughs that had once been cake stands. Their playing cards were mostly torn up and used as tapers, and the house itself crumbled and fell almost imperceptibly under the drifting sand.

Once again, the family had virtually died out, and once again there was a great quantity of chipped and broken porcelain scattered over the land. The valley was covered with the brightly coloured chips of china and a layer of despair. After the death of the two sisters the drought took over where Sara Beltrán had let go, it squeezed all the life out of the land, and it brought ruin and disease that was carried in dirty water. The drought squeezed so hard that those who stayed were not merely survivors, but combatants. There was the land, and the drought itself, and Lydia Sinclair who was pregnant, and her husband Diego who was paralysed, and there was Cristóbal Beltrán who was ageless and all-knowing and indestructible. It was Cristóbal who sifted the sand in the hourglass, and it was he who had signalled fat Rosa Beltrán to die.

Epilogue

I

O N the third morning after old Benito's death, Lydia awoke feeling more tired and cramped than ever before. It was dawn of 3rd September, 1962, and she lay back, enjoying the short respite from the sun: the early morning was the only time when the high altitude of the surrounding hills could defy the climate. The sun was slowly climbing over the mountains, and soon the still, airless heat of every day would take over, flaying the fissured skin of the valley once more. She eased herself down from the high, mahogany bed inlaid with satinwood and, dressing quietly, she left her husband, Diego, sleeping in his massive immobility. She paused in the doorway for a while to watch his inert body in its seventh month of paralysis, and its second year in bed. His hair and beard had grown long and grey, making him look more than ever like his distant cousin, Cristóbal, who still limped by their house every day.

From the wide balcony that adjoined their suite of rooms, she could see the thick dead leaves of the malaguetta tree, whose aromatic leaves sweetened the air, and the brittle remains of tangled jasmine; and to the far side of the house, at the foot of the nearest hill, there was a single row of palm trees each older and taller than the next, and each with a cluster of withered fruits high in its crown. There was one tree planted for each Beltrán born on the Hacienda: there was one for Rodrigo, and one for each of his sons, one for Alejandro and Elías, one for Diego, and one for her own dead son. These palm trees were not native to the Andes, but brought up from the coastal plains, and they unfurled like flags of defiance. In the last four years they had begun to flourish as never before. They thrived on the drought and the drifting sand, basking in the heat that they had so patiently awaited; and, amid the autumn colours of other scorched and dying trees, and the charred remains of fires, they retained their green shimmer and bore fruit. Lydia saw, with regret, that now even these palm trees had shrivelled, and their branches lay strewn like bonfires of bracken around their fraying trunks.

Downstairs in the kitchen she made some coffee and then leant on the balustrade overlooking the road, and watched for Cristóbal to come limping into view. Her coffee was thick and muddy, and, like everything else in the house, it tasted of weevils. Yet, that day, it tasted especially good to her, in the knowledge that it would be the last cup of coffee that she would drink there: it was her last day on the Hacienda. After three days and nights of work, she had finally managed to assemble and equip one complete jeep from the fleet of broken cars in the stables. As she stood there, looking down the valley, her bones ached at the thought of not seeing Cristóbal once more before she left.

It was eight o'clock before she saw the familiar vultures heralding his approach. Then he followed, close behind, leaning on his staff. As he neared the archway where Lydia stood, she tried to imprint on her mind every rag and detail of him for future reference. She memorised his dishevelled mane of grizzled hair, and the ragged stump of his mutilated leg. When she herself left later on that day, taking her paralysed husband, Diego, with her, and carrying her unborn child, Cristóbal would be the last Beltrán left in the valley, and (possibly) the last man. But he had been there for so long that he almost was the valley. Benito had said that he remembered him as old when he himself was still a boy. He had patrolled the banks of the Momboy for over a hundred years. He moved like a pendulum in an endless coming and going, and he became so regular a feature that he seemed like the land itself. Even death had not overtaken him as it did other men: his age was not a mortal age. In all he did he was unusual – he swung between extremes, refusing to pause;

and, unlike others, he would never die in any way that involved the usual phase from death to decomposition. He would not die, but fade away with the valley itself, and together they would drift into sand. The drought was watering his blood, and he could feel its steady advance clogging his veins. His mass of beard and hair was as scorched and brittle as the last charred weeds, and his once ruddy complexion was burnt to dry flakes that fell in his wake.

Lydia watched him coming towards her that morning, like a slow ghost. His clothes seemed more torn than ever, and the string that held up his trousers was torn and trailing. Benito had told her the story of this giant scarecrow, and of his lameness, many times, and yet its strangeness never ceased to surprise her. Cristóbal was the third son of Ernesto, who had been both Minister of Finance in Caracas and a famous judge in Trujillo. When Cristóbal was six, his mother died while giving birth to a baby brother who also died, and his father retired with his grief to the capital, neglecting his three remaining sons in favour of his former career.

The two elder boys ruled the household and the family's estates with fanatical authority. Their premature burdens had made them unusually self-conscious, and they would tolerate no flexibility in their reign of terror. They sensed that some of their former power was slipping from their grasp; the River Momboy seemed to be washing away the customs and beliefs of their workers, and they saw it as their duty to set a solid example. However, Cristóbal could not be brought to understand this. The welts of their whip made no impression on his mind, and the more they punished him, the more his physical condition deteriorated, and the less he repented.

After their father's death, Cristóbal's refusal to conform seemed to insult them personally. Perhaps what most angered them was the knowledge that this brother possessed energy such as they could never even hope to feel – the boy had the unchanneled strength of a pacing tiger. They believed that if only he could be made to conform, he would not only cease to embarrass them, but also attain

great heights. Yet he was stubborn and wayward, and he strayed
from home. He was otherwise sweet-natured and amenable in all
things save in his insistence on his freedom to wander the hills.
Cristóbal claimed that he could not breathe unless he roamed so,
and he complained of fever in his body when he stayed still. There
was a wave of restlessness that welled up inside him like physical
pain that roaming alone could ease. So he never stayed long at
home, and could not sit still; he frequently missed his mealtimes,
and constantly ran away from his tutor. Cristóbal ignored his punished and battered flesh, and he ignored his brothers' wrath, and
every morning he would set out for yet another day of rambling
on the hills.

Cristóbal grew somehow, despite his solitude; and, in lieu of
any family love, after his mother's death, he turned to the hills.
For at the age of six, he, who had been his mother's pet, became a
scapegoat for everybody's grief. Instead of soothing his own sense
of lack, his brothers somehow blamed him, the youngest, for the
loss of their mother: they had been very close to her too and now
all that was left them was this whining child. His cousins came,
from the Hacienda La Bebella, and offered to take him and bring
him up with their own young sons. But Cristóbal's father would
have none of it – he must stay with his brothers, who would be an
example to him. Thus he was left to mourn alone, and only the hills
were there to cradle him and fill his sense of loss. He grew up there,
on the highlands, on the borders of the cold *páramo*; and from the
outcrops of rock that he climbed, he could survey the whole valley
stretching out below; and it was then that he swore his allegiance
to the hills that had become his only solace.

His brothers tried everything to keep him at home. They kept
him for months on cornbread soaked in milk, allowing him no
meat or beans or coffee. They confiscated his books, and forbade
him to visit his cousins; they set him extra tasks and lessons, and
they beat him until their own arms ached, and his skin was black

and blue. His face often bore the shadow of faded rainbows rippling on his cheeks as he blinked, and the blues and greens and yellows shifted under his skin and over the bumps and contusions that their many blows produced – and still he would pay them no heed. They locked him in his room, but he escaped through his barred window, leaving a wreckage of splintered wood behind him. They locked him naked in his room – yet still he escaped, and found clothes. They locked him in a windowless room, with no clothes and no light, and he nearly died there, plagued by insects and his festering sores. Then the servants told the villagers, and the villagers complained,

'Beat the boy, cleanly, but don't torment him.'

And it was in the light of this interference that his brothers' anger turned cruel. They would force him to conform. Even the vultures in the sky seemed to say,

'¿Qué dirán? ¿Qué dirán?'

And Cristóbal's two brothers knew well what their neighbours were saying; they would be holding them to ridicule; they would be whispering behind their backs that they could not control this wayward child. But they, too, would see. They would all see what real authority could be. It was his feet that offended them – so they would punish his feet.

They burned the sole of his right foot with a white-hot cattle iron. At fifteen, Cristóbal had the strength of a wrestler, and it took some time for him to slump into a pale sweat of pain, so the iron was driven in, further, perhaps, than had been intended. His foot was branded deep into the flesh, scorching a piece of bone as the whole room filled with the smoke.

Cristóbal lay salved and bandaged in his bed for five long days until a restlessness drove him back to the hills. It was they alone that could cool his blood and ease what seemed like ice grating over his wound. Every cell in his body was singed; it was as though the back of his head had opened up, revealing the inside of his skull; and his brain was sucking and swallowing directly from his surroundings, without the usual mediation of his nervous system. The whole world was crawling into his head – settling in this or that lobe, fitting into the fissures and lumps. Cristóbal stood in his massive beauty on the hilltops; and the frangipani trees, the bucare and black cedars seemed to sit under his crown, and they sheltered him during the hardest moments of his unhealed wound and his strange self-trepanation. The thin scabs on his foot tore open, and the flesh became swollen beyond all recognition. The edges gaped and oozed, and he was pursued by the clinging smell of infected burns that filled the air, following him like a river of sewage wherever he went. Undaunted, he stripped a thick staff, and took to the mountains like a wounded bear.

It was old Benito's father, Lisandro, who had healed his foot, long before Benito himself was born; he had bathed it with a solution of wild rosemary and salt that stung on the cuts. He bandaged Cristóbal with cool fibrous palm leaves, and lowered his fever as he lay on a woven mat on the floor of his smoke-grimed hut. Each day, Cristóbal lay on his own, waiting for the man to return from his work, laden with odds and ends that he had picked up on the way, such as vultures' eggs for supper, or a pocketful of tiny rose-scented plums that grew wild in the surrounding woods. Sometimes he would bring back a chip of porcelain or a rattling clay doll made and buried by the Indians centuries before. The fields were full of relics, and this man had his own special way of explaining their presence, more enthralling by far than that of Cristóbal's former tutor.

Only one theme had ever interested Cristóbal in the long imprisonment of his lessons. He had had no time for theology or mathematics or Latin grammar: he was interested only in history. He had sat for hours listening to even his boring tutor come alive as he told the story of his namesake, Cristóbal Colón, and his discovery of America. His own ancestors had come, on the third of these voyages, stopping first at the island of Hispaniola, and then sailing onto the mainland. They had come with the vision of the great future of El Dorado, and a desire to be present during its rise to glory – they themselves would guide its course whilst thriving on its riches. And they had stayed, the de Labastidas and the Briceños, the Aragóns and the Gabaldóns and the de Melos. But Cristóbal felt a strange mixture of these ancestral feelings: he foresaw a continued rise in the fortunes of the valley, but he also saw the ravages of its decline. The land would slowly turn to dust, and Cristóbal determined to be present when the drought that his thoughts prophesied took a stranglehold on the hills and plains, and throttled every last drop of life from his homeland.

No one else had any idea of what was to come: they did not know that their ordered society would crumble like a pack of cards. The black vomit, the Massacre, the famine and the drought would all come by surprise; no one would believe in them until their force had undermined the land. Everything was to change: only Cristóbal would be there – as the one constant amidst the upheavals and the decay. Cristóbal would be to the valley what the hills had been to him.

II

It was not long before his brothers found him, and when they did, they had lost every Christian feeling in them, and all their natural pity had drained with their loss of pride. They spoke with their jaws set in a rigid grimace. Old Benito's father was turned out of his hut and off their estates. He loaded his mule with his belongings, and he journeyed away from the uplands and the *páramo* where he had been born, and travelled down to the neighbouring lands and hills which belonged to Cristóbal's ageing cousin, known as El General-ísimo. The two brothers kept back ropes and an axe from their departing worker, and when he was gone, they bound Cristóbal to a long wooden bench. They had brought their cattle branding iron with them, and they put it in the fire on the deserted hearth. Cristóbal said nothing – too shocked by the sudden departure of his new-found friend. From the moment that Benito's father set off down the track with his overloaded mule, and his heavy sackful of stones and trinkets, Cristóbal felt a final severing of his family tie. What was to follow was merely the confirmation of what he felt: they were all strangers. And then and there, Cristóbal renounced the lands that were his inheritance, forfeiting his wealth, denying kinship to the many different branches of his family, shunning all human company, speaking to no one, no matter whom, choosing rather to patrol the banks of the Momboy, watching and waiting.

When the iron was hot, and the two brothers impatient, one of them took the axe and the other the brand. Then the rough blade, ground on a weathered whetstone, swung down and shattered the boy's flesh and bone, while the other brother rammed the red-hot iron onto the spurting pulp and cauterised the wound. Cristóbal had seen the hatred in his brothers' eyes, and he had seen the scraped blade catch the light as it fell, then he too had fallen after the first flicker of pain. When he came to, strapped down by leather thongs to his own bed in his brothers' house, he was still falling, and only the edges of his bed were there – the rest had slipped away. He was aware of a gnawing pain in his right foot – the old burn in his sole was nagging him. It was only after the delirium faded that he realised that he had no foot to ache, and that the whole of his right leg had gone, amputated to the upper thigh.

The household was hushed, and the servants rustled in and out of his room with pails and swabs, and he guessed the censor of his mutilation in their red eyes and sullen faces. In their world, there was no place for the maimed, and death was preferable to disablement. Such things, they knew, could not happen further down the valley: it was here, on the uplands, that the cold wind had warped their brains. One by one the peasants left, heading for La Bebella, and the lowlands. Meanwhile, Cristóbal healed and hardened his ungainly stump, and, choosing a strong staff as tall as a vaulting pole, he swung himself away from his brothers' house, determined never to return. The rest of his life was entirely dedicated to patrolling the crumpled foothills for a distance of some twenty miles, from the market town of La Caldera to the small mountain village of Timotes and back again. His itinerary was as regular as a railway train, and his staff and one foot furrowed the track of the Camino Real.

III

Lydia felt so reluctant to leave the Hacienda that her every move-ment had become slow and ineffectual. Each trip to the jeep and back was taking an unusually long time. Her feet dragged as she walked, willing her to stay; there even seemed to be a shimmer of life on the parched slopes, and she could have sworn that there were birds other than birds of prey in the fields around her. But it was merely the sun catching on skulls and stones or dry gourds, hanging from the telegraph wires or knotted around dead trees. The only live beings left were herself and Diego, and their dog, and Cristóbal, and the turkey vultures frantic for Benito's corpse. Ever since she had left his barrow-like grave to make her preparations, the vultures had landed there, grappling and scratching at the stone until their own beaks tore and bled – but they could not budge the mound of heavy rock that Lydia had laid there. She knew that they would try to get her husband, Diego, when she brought him down, because he too seemed lifeless, and they would sense the death in him. She found an old tarpaulin to wrap him in, like a winding sheet, to shield him from their horny beaks.

Cristóbal was sitting outside her house, on the road, leaning against a rough milestone. Over his shoulder she could still decipher the familiar number chipped out of the white rock: four hundred – it was four hundred miles to the capital, four hundred miles to the sea, and more than four hundred years since the first of the family came searching for gold. Now only Cristóbal remained, who had limited the roundness of his world and its discovery to the pacing of the whittled slopes and their disastrous erosion. And it struck her that his appearance was as strange to herself and her peers as that of Cortés and his men had been to the astonished Aztecs on their arrival in Mexico. Lydia felt her child stir in her womb, and struggled to complete her preparations. Meanwhile, Cristóbal stayed down on the road, surveying what was left of the house and lands of La Bebella.

At times he shifted his gaze from the stone balustrade where Lydia had been leaning, turning his eyes alternately to the once seething town of La Caldera, and, in the other direction, to the chill uplands where he had been born. Lydia climbed the uneven staircase to her library, where legions of cockroaches had feasted, reducing it all to shreds and dust, and she watched Cristóbal's every movement through the dull cedar doors that led out onto one of the many balconies.

The house was built along three sides of a square; Diego lay as though in state at one end, and she stood at the other, looking out at Cristóbal and the caked remains of the River Momboy, and, beyond them, the disused factory and mill. One side of the house lay open, and the high whitewashed corridors all led directly onto what used to be a formal rose garden enclosed by high gates and a wall. But now the gates hung awkwardly on their hinges, and the gaps that they made in the courtyard wall were like unhealed wounds through which the displaced sand and decay swept in and stayed.

The burnt orange tiles of the uneven roof flared like bonfires in the sky. Lydia looked down the long quadrangle of flames, and the tightness in her brain shrank from the roofs furnace. She had still to fetch one of the tiles from the old floor of gold and pack it safely in the jeep, and she had still somehow to carry Diego down the main stairs. The library, which was really two large rooms, had been her tower, her solace now for ten long years. The cracks in the walls were full of her whisperings, and the hollow beams and bats' nests under the boards knew how much she missed all that was lost and gone. The whole room seemed to weep and sigh in echo to her sorrow.

And yet, she thought, would ten years seem a long time to Cristóbal? She decided that it would, but she did not know how long. She didn't know that under his immutable mask every day was one of torment. Nor did she realise quite how much he suffered from his ill-severed limb, nor how the valley's death was his own slow dying. With all the diligence of a natural farmer, he had roamed landless through the valley, observing every blade and detail of the hills and fields that he knew so well. Even when the crops had grown easily, he had foreseen the time when the hills would become barren and deserted, and deserts would shape themselves where there had been woods. And he himself would finally wither and dry so much that not even the vultures would stay for him, and he would fade into the mist of dry ashes, and be covered over by sand.

When the locusts came, he alone had known that the famine would pass. Afterwards, he had pitied La Comadre Matilde with her premonitions of destruction. She had urged every family she could reach to fear the land, little knowing that the land itself would also be destroyed. He had watched the frail hut of Matilde's blind aunt over the years. A young girl used to tend to the old woman's needs; and he remembered her in the rain. He could remember vividly what the valley used to be like when it rained – it seemed to wash off caked mud and release new possibilities of movement. When it rained, the whole world relaxed.

With the first warm drops a bout of almost clockwork bustle would break through their routines. In every hut and household, preparations were made for the forthcoming downpour. There was a rush for pails and pans to catch the drops, shutters were drawn, and the bunches of beans, hung over poles to dry, were covered. Mounds of coffee were hauled into outhouses, and the multi-coloured flags of drying clothes were jumbled together and stuffed into hammocks. Then everyone would sit back, and an undertow of well-being needled its way through their veins. The rain came in a distemper of relief, and not all those who heralded the first showers were there to wave out the last. There were always some of the very old and young who succumbed to the colds and fevers of the rains, and those who died of the many forms of dysentery that the wet weather brought in its tow. In the days when it rained regularly, and each year was divided into two seasons, the dry and the wet, the month of May was the wettest. And there was even a name for the illness that came at that time – it was called the *mayera* – and it appeared in the records as the cause of death of many a child.

La Comadre Matilde's aunt grew older, and the cataracts over her blind eyes grew bluer, and yet she did not die. Cristóbal remembered how he had walked by one afternoon and seen her slumped against the limed wall of her cluttered veranda. She had been hauled out there by the girl who nursed her, and her cloths and petticoats were draped around her to dry. As signs of a storm gathered overhead, her nurse had run home to help seal up her own hut, and the old woman had lain huddled and silent under her canopy of damp laundry. Her legs had grown as pale and bony as an old woman's legs can grow under the waxen knots of arthritis. She had been taken out with the washing and everyone had forgotten to take her in. Her knees and wrists were too weak to help her crawl more than a few feet, and she could not find her own door. She called to the girl, who was far away and out of earshot; and she called to Matilde, who was nowhere near; but all that came by way of reply was the rumbling of the storm, and rain so hard that it scarcely let her breathe. When she opened her mouth to cry out, the fat drops of water threatened to drown her like a duck. She had watched ducks drown, many times, in their own element. They lifted their necks as though to give thanks for the rain, and, opening their throats in adoration, the rainwater choked them. So the old woman ceased to call, muttering instead at her niece's neglect. In the long hours of her drenching, she cursed Matilde – who would have lain down her life for her. And she cursed her indifference – even though she cared for no one but this one blind aunt.

Matilde never knew how harshly her absence had been taken that day. Nor did she know that her aunt became a child again as she lay battened to the ground and beaten by hour upon hour of heavy rain. Only Cristóbal saw her skinny bones and skull plastered to the floor at the mercy of the tempest and her truant nurse. He foresaw that the girl would come and haul her in again, and he foresaw that much later the old woman would die despite Matilde's broths and pains; and he knew that her body would be a mere heap of deranged swellings, and that Matilde would be lost without her.

IV

Cristóbal looked around him, surveying the extent of the drought. The vultures were nowhere to be seen, and he guessed that they would be trying to scratch up old Benito. Up in the big house he saw Lydia trying to close the library doors, and caught a glimpse of her as she walked slowly towards Diego's room. He, Cristóbal, had not seen his cousin Diego for years, but in his mind's eye he could see him lying still on his bed, and he sensed that inside Diego's head there was the same shrinking feeling as in his own, except that the back of his own head was prised permanently open.

Lydia opened both sides of the double doors that led to Diego's room, then she took a pile of clothes from the drawers and shelves of his makeshift dressing room and carried them to his bed. It seemed impossible to her that it was only less than nine months ago that she had stood in a similar position in her study, and he had called out to her, gripped by a stroke, and after that he had not spoken or moved again. Only the bulge of her pregnancy was there to authenticate the fact that Diego had not always been so helpless. All his work and thoughts and dreams were scattered and buried in the empty fields, and no one would ever know – to look at him now – how very nearly he had saved the valley. No one man had worked harder to keep the river flowing. He had treated the land with all the respect that was its due. He had sown a whole revolution of methods and technique. He had terraced the hillslope to stop the erosion, and added calcium and phosphates to the soil; he had made the Hacienda rich in nitrates, and the green leaves became as green as they had been a hundred years before.

Diego had fought the forest fires and the felling of trees, and he had fought the inertia that idleness had planted in every field. He had fought more as an hacendado than as an idealist; some of the townspeople had refused to mourn his father's death, and he had not risked his life to better theirs, but to save the land itself. Before he met Lydia, he had worked to overthrow the Government, and it was through his subsequent exile that they had first met in London.

For over half a century, a chain of corrupt governments had ruined the countryside, systematically vandalising and neglecting the land and destroying all its natural resources. They cared only for the oil beds at Maracaibo and along the Orinoco. Like María Candelaria they would do anything for glitter. Under their callous eyes, estates were abandoned and rivers dried. They didn't need trees anymore; they had the exotic fruits that were ferried daily from Mexico and Miami. They lured the peasants off the land and into the cities where they went hungry while the fields stood bare. They tyrannised the country's economy with their transitory oil. But in recent years there had been only one rule: that of the drought. The drought dictated, and the land obeyed. The soil refused to be renewed, and the river denied its abundance. Field after field surrendered and lay cracked and fallow under the taunting sun. Even the prickly weeds that had bristled here and there shed their thistles and burrs and died, and their seeds were barren.

Lydia dressed her husband as best she could, raising his body under the knees to ease his weight. He lay like a thirteenth-century Spanish king, his face so pale that it glowed, and with the sad eyes of a spaniel. She dressed him in the traditional cream linen suit that had long gone out of fashion; she was sure that Diego would have liked to have left his home thus, in what was once the national dress. Then, from his grandfather's dusty writing box she took the family signet ring. This ring was always passed from eldest son to eldest son, and Diego was the last of these heirs by direct descent of primogeniture. One of his hands was beginning to wither, but the other was still as delicate and firm as ever. He had wanted to be a concert pianist, and as a child he had loved to play his favourites in alternating hours, lulling the house between Chopin's sonatas and the tremor of Tchaikovsky's first piano concerto. He had had a natural flair, but when he was twelve his mother forbade him ever to touch the instrument again, and the grand piano was banished from the drawing room to the bat droppings in the stables and then finally given to the Home for Unmarried Mothers. Diego's mother maintained that it was both unmanly and unnatural for a boy to be a pianist. Even now, on the verge of middle age, Diego still listened in glazed rapture to the First Concerto, which Lydia played again and again for him until the record was worn to a smooth sheet of black plastic and the music was blurred to a mere series of louder notes interspersed with a slow whirring.

Diego rarely mentioned his mother, they shared nothing but their name and blood and their financial gullibility. She had died ten years after his father, on a skiing trip to Bariloche, and out of loyalty to him Diego preferred not to remember her faults, parrying all Lydia's questions with a firm,

'He loved her.'

Diego had always been his father's child, and no one else's. Lydia knew that it was time to take him downstairs, and she went down herself to fetch the tarpaulin to wrap him in. Looking up at the sky, she saw that it was already ten o'clock, she would have to hurry – Cristóbal was waiting for her.

V

When she had first arrived, the children in the Hacienda had called Cristóbal 'El Coco', the Wild One. He never spoke or begged, and he was angered by any interference, however kindly it was meant. Nobody knew what he ate, or how he lived, and few remembered who he was. His hair was full of lice, and his clothes were tattered – he had chosen to live outside their society, and there was no place for him. He passed mostly unnoticed as he trudged the many miles from La Caldera to the uplands. He had wended his way through the coffee groves with their shading palms, and he had seen them give way to sugarcane. Then he had wended his way through the mills and factories and the long trains of donkeys. Under the hill-fragmented sun, he had wended his way through the disused chimneys that towered over the bucare and the bracken. He had patrolled the Momboy valley through its transition from richness to ruin.

In his head he had charted a map, and like Cristóbal Colón, he was obsessed by his voyages. His Indies were the Andes of his birth, and his Spain was the Hacienda La Bebella. He could traffic neither gold nor precious stones between the two, but he carried comfort, and his very presence was the stump and vestige of loyalty. He sought no reward, roaming entirely from vocation. Cristóbal wondered if Lydia knew that she was the last person to survive;

even her farm was one of the last to die. Higher up the valley, the drought had wiped out every plot and homestead many years before.

He remembered the bluish hue of their cabbage patches between the bald rocks. Every pocket of land that had any topsoil at all was farmed and the farmers trailed behind their ploughs, sharing the yoke with their lumpy-skinned oxen. The men who farmed the uplands lived a spartan life, and it had always been their own hard work that kept them alive. But when the drought came, no amount of work could save their crops. The mounds of compost that they dug into the earth dried and were swept away by the wind into drifts and furrows. Even the climate changed, and the potatoes that they planted refused to grow without the frosts and mists of before. On their chiselled plateaux the farmers laboured under woollen cloaks to help the dry soil to yield its withered leaves, and they refused steadfastly to lay down these cloaks, thereby admitting their defeat, so they denied both the heat and their sorrow. Their sons would never know a real harvest – just the stunted uneven tubers that they ate and saved. The barrels and chests that they had filled half-yearly for so many years were slowly emptied to eke out their losing battle. Bewildered by the changes and the wanton squandering of their resources, they harrowed and waited, broadcasting their fears to the wind and the rocks, and drink became their only solace.

They drank to drown their exhaustion and to ease their loss, and they drank sadly to the birth of their children, knowing that their inheritance would come from the lowlands and not from them. They were filled with guilt at having sired them, and so laid them bare to disaster. They wasted and dried into straggling scarecrows, and they combed the hills, reaping their meagre fruit and a heritage of fire. As though the drought were not enough, there were rings of fire on every horizon, and they were forced to farm between the half-circles of ashes and clinker, tending weeds with the same determination with which they had once pulled them out.

They drank until they were numb in their empty stables, and then they staggered home, past the low roofs of the empty deposits where their potato crops had been stored and sacked. Everything was a had-been: they lurched through a fog of had-beens, until the fog was inside their bleary heads. It was not the same fog that had mystified their youth and chilblained their fingers; it was a heavy green-wood smoke that choked and stuck. Life itself was a slow process for them, and Cristóbal remembered with what relief they had died. Death alone released them from the long war in which they would not surrender, and which they could not win. They passed, like him, mostly unnoticed, since their relations were too crazed and dried to cry, and only cobwebs sat like gossamer on their rough-hewn coffins in lieu of tears, and solanum grew from their graves. He had trampled the deadly nightshade and prodded the belladonna with his staff many times, and they lay in one of his favourite cemeteries, outside the mountain village of Timotes.

VI

The sun was moving steadily across the charred slopes, and Lydia needed no dial to see that she would have to hurry. Even if the roads were still in fair condition, it would take her from twelve to twenty hours to reach the sea. The back of the jeep was stacked with cans of petrol, water and gourds. The battered canvas roof was stretched and tied in position, and her old Winchester rifle lay across the front seat, together with a small Colt revolver, and a sawn-off double-barrelled shotgun. The glove compartment was well-stocked with cartridges, and she had packed matches and string, food and knives, and such spare parts as she deemed necessary. All she needed now was to fetch Diego.

She felt that the vultures were watching her too closely, so she dropped her bundle of canvas and picked up the rifle, and pressing the butt hard against her shoulder, she took her aim and shot down one of the birds, and the others all flapped after it, squabbling in a frenzy of torn feathers. Now Lydia knew that she would have the time it took them to pick clean its bones to carry her husband downstairs. All that was left were the stairs. Lydia had been avoiding them all morning. They implied too definite a finality. They had assumed massive proportions in her mind, and become almost too high to climb. When she first arrived in the house, she had been unusually impressed by their size and splendour, and their mottled green marble was engraved in her head. Even the stairs held many memories, and the slight dips in the treads were worn by her own and others' feet through centuries of routine.

But Diego was neither to walk nor fall down these stairs as so many others had done before him. He would descend quite differently: he would be hauled down by Lydia. His body was too heavy for her even to attempt to carry, and now especially she could risk no miscarriage, so she wrapped him in the old tarpaulin and dragged him down. She held his shoulders and let his legs trail and bump on the treads. He descended like the dead General after the Massacre, and Lydia was the only one left to help him. There was no banister, and it was all that Lydia could do to keep from falling. She winced as Diego's body hit the steps, and she could almost feel him bruising.

She felt too sad now to look at the faded portraits on the walls, and she ignored the row of closed doors that she passed as she laboured with Diego's weight. His body had left a wide track through the dust and sand. She passed the doors like so many splinters of a salt-fish bone: there were the marble sitting-room and the guest room, the toy room and the ever-empty nursery, the study and Matilde's room, the store room, pantry and kitchen, the dining room and the suite of halls with their high arches leading onto each other, all fanning off one side of the spine, while the wide, pillared veranda led onto a completely dead inner garden and groves of lifeless trees.

The house had become the bubble of an hourglass and the tall gate, its waist. Sand drifted in from the hacienda to the halls in a steady trickle until the fields seemed empty, and the house full. There was nothing left to do, and Lydia had always hated good-byes. She heaped Diego's body into the back of the jeep as best she could, finding that one half of him invariably slipped down once she had got the other half in. But after some tugging and pulling, she succeeded in wedging him between the seats. Cristóbal was still down on the road to the side of the house, and therefore could not see herñ but Megan, her last beagle hound, had been staring through the bars of the study window at her. There was a look of both longing and confidence in the dog's eyes, and she hurried her thin ribs across the hall, and scrambled into the back seat, twisting and turning around Diego's face, until she had found a comfortable space for herself

Megan was Lydia's one compatriot in that strange and newly barren land: she had sailed with her from England ten years before, crated in a sheep pen on the upper deck of the Montserrat, the Spanish ship that had rocked them across the Atlantic. Her coat was dull now, and her ears and haunches scarred by the ravages of sores and worms, and she was a mere shadow of the show champion she had once been. When the drought began, Megan had begun her own campaign: she became an expert at finding food and she grew fat on lizards, geckos and flies. She would eat any number of flies, and later she thrived on the watery beans, palm slime and weevils.

Once they were all in, Lydia started the engine. She had started it several times the day before, but even so she held her breath, in case it would not go. Then, with only one last look back, she drove down the bumpy, almost impassable track to the road. The jeep lurched, and her two passengers were thrown from side to side against the fastened cans of petrol. Halfway down, the wheels stuck in a drift of sand, and she had to work with her hands and a shovel to clear the way. The drive from the house to the road was just under a mile long, and lined with dead avocado trees. When she finally reached the road, Cristóbal had already risen, and was walking away uphill. She could see only the back of his head with its massive mane of hair and his staff which gave him an almost supernatural height. Ahead of him flew a straggling band of vultures, which turned to follow her as she drove away. They seemed to know that Cristóbal would not die, but slowly desiccate, and the drought in their gullets bade them turn tail and follow Lydia and the Beltráns.

VII

Lydia drove on to the town of La Caldera, stopping only once to shoot down one of the troop of vultures to decoy its brothers from Diego and herself. She passed the Plaza Bolívar, and the other square with its statue of General Mario and its derelict mansions; and she passed street after deserted street of rubble and clay. Even the cathedral had broken doors and windows, and what looked like a sand dune in its open aisle. The covered marketplace flapped shreds of coloured canvas and the looted stalls were overturned. There were pieces of bone and skull in the most unexpected places, and many of the doors on many of the houses were barricaded and marked with a black cross as though for plague. The whole place was desolate. Lydia left the town behind her, and the cemetery that hemmed its outskirts, overflowing in endless skimped additions. Then the road took her downhill, past a disused barracks, to a wide bridge across the dry bed of the River Momboy, and she climbed once more with the road, to the hill that lay outside the town of La Caldera. It was a suddenly high place in the slow descent to the sea, and because there had once been a prison there, it was known by the name of Calvary. Lydia shot down one more vulture, buying her own time with its death; and, keeping her engine running, she stepped down for a moment to take one last look at the valley she was about to leave.

As she faced the highlands, she could see, to her right, the stone wall of the barracks of Escuque where the Massacre had taken place, and high on a hill above it, outlined against the sky, was the skeleton of the magnolia tree that Diego's grandfather had planted there as a token of thanks to the people who had helped him. Then, to her left, she saw the tall flue of her own mill chimney in the sun. It was the tallest chimney of its time in the Andes, and it stood like a cenotaph to all those who had given their lives to the Hacienda. Then, last of all, she saw Cristóbal standing on a distant outcrop like a statue of rock; and the sun seemed to shine directly upon him so that his shock of wild hair became a blaze of gold, and around his head there was a strange halo.

Despite the distance, Lydia could see him very clearly, more clearly, in fact, than ever before, and it seemed to her suddenly that the halo was composed entirely of splintered bones. He turned and walked away, taking with him his strange headdress of a lifetime's hunger; for the bones were the discarded bones of the salt fish they had all eaten in the times of plenty; and they were the bones that yellowed nails had dug for, when the drought began, to boil again; and they were the bones that old men had sucked and dribbled as they chewed their cud of thistles. They were all of their bones, and they were splinters of china, and hidden wishbones too, and Cristóbal had been storing them in his trepanned head for a long time. And now there was no one left to see, he had shaken them loose, and Lydia's last vision of the valley was of this one mutilated man whose strength of mind and body dominated the land as surely as his forefathers had done before him. He was a part of the hills themselves: the hot sands would bury him, and only then would he lay down his staff and end his marathon. Meanwhile, Lydia felt the child in her womb turn and slide until the weight of its head rested in the cavity of her groin, and it seemed symbolic that it should have been so crowned before leaving the land of its ancestors; and it seemed like a good sign for her child who was thus laden with history even before it was born.

New from Lisa St Aubin de Terán

Better Broken than New

Following a successful career as an award-winning, best-selling novelist, in 2004 Lisa St Aubin de Terán retreated to a remote village in northern Mozambique. There she found her own African roots, founded a charity, and confronted new challenges. Much has been written about her life and escapades with a trio of Venezuelan exiles, life on an Andean hacienda, her return to literary fame, and two decades living in a crumbling Umbrian palace. But despite all the media hype about her, she managed to hide much of her actual life.

Now, like the Japanese art of kintsugi, in this new memoir Lisa puts the shattered pieces of her life back together, filling in many of the dramatic, and often scandalous, gaps. While her life has been said to be stranger than fiction, it is fiction that has kept her afloat. This autobiography sets the record straight and shows a writer who for over half a century has enjoyed following her dreams, even when those dreams outdistanced her reach.

Published by Amaurea Press, January 2024
hardback ISBN 9781914278129 (£19.95/€22.95/$24.95)
eBook ISBN 9781914278143 (£4.99/€5.99/$6.99)

Coming 2024
A new novel by Lisa St Aubin de Terán

The Hobby

When police pay a visit to an elderly peeping tom, they unexpectedly stumble upon a loose thread that leads detective John Custer into a murky world of sex crimes and serial killings, of hidden graves and socially impeccable paedophiles. Ignoring the scepticism of his colleagues and superiors, Custer doggedly follows his intuition that there really is something very wrong that needs to be discovered, however cold the trail seems to have become.

Based upon a true story of a bizarre and tragic case of child abuse, *The Hobby* is a psychological crime thriller, ranging from the fan club of a 1940s child star, through Istanbul and war-torn Burma and Cairo, to 1980s Britain. Custer and his assistant, Sergeant Jolly Campbell, seek to bring justice to the forgotten victims, while themselves going through their own quest for personal redemption.

hardback ISBN 9781914278396
eBook ISBN 9781914278402

amaurea

New Amaurea Press editions of the books of Lisa St Aubin de Terán

The Slow Train to Milan

ISBN 9781914278181 (hbk), 9781914278198 (pbk), 9781914278204 (ebk)

To Lisaveta, César remained as much of an enigma after two years of their nomadic exile together as he had that first day in Clapham when he showed no signs of shifting out of her life, ever. But why were César and his friends Otto and Elías on the run, and from whom? From London, they drifted south from Paris to Milan and back – stopping at Bologna, Grenoble, Venice – wherever the slow train takes them.

Winner of the John Llewellyn Rhys Prize

The Tiger

ISBN 9781914278211 (hbk), 9781914278228 (pbk), 9781914278235 (ebk)

The servants said that even the waters of the Orinoco obeyed Misia Schmutter, the white-haired old lady, so proud of her Prussian ancestry, who treated the world like her slave. She had seen a glint of her own ruthlessness in her grandson Lucien's eye. Worshipping and torturing him by turns she cultivated in him a terrible understanding of tyranny and the true nature of power.

The Bay of Silence

ISBN 9781914278242 (hbk), 9781914278259 (pbk), 9781914278266 (ebk)

It all appears innocent enough: a handsome couple revisting the Italian Riviera. But they are driven by paranoia – by a slow dread of what will happen to them and their daughters if anyone finds out about their baby, whose identity and existence is at the heart of the schizophrenia from which Rosalind has long suffered.

www.amaurea.co.uk

Milton Keynes UK
Ingram Content Group UK Ltd.
UKHW012101150124
436101UK00016B/253/J